SHE LEFT THE BABIES IN THE BED

FAMILY SCANDAL LOST TO HISTORY FOR OVER 100 YEARS

ELAINE CRUME

ILLUMIFY
MEDIA.COM

CONTENTS

She Left the Babies in the Bed

Published by
Illumify Media Global
www.IllumifyMedia.com
"We bring your book to life!"

Library of Congress Control Number: 2021909333

Paperback ISBN: 978-1-955043-02-1
eBook ISBN: 978-1-955043-03-8

Typeset by Jennifer Clark
Cover design by Debbie Lewis

Printed in the United States of America

To Larry Yoder, my touchstone. Je t'aime pour toujours.

Life hinges around singular moments, words spoken that set the tone for everything that comes after. Some of those moments leave scars on the soul forever.

ONE

MONDAY'S CHILD IS FAIR OF FACE

IT WAS TOLD to me like this. She left the babies in the bed and ran off with a salesman. It was a shocking piece of ancient gossip provided to me with great delight by a distant cousin. When he first divulged the story of our mutual relative, Lydia Ross McGee had been lying dead in an unvisited grave for over a hundred years. Old news indeed, but she was kin and I was intrigued. The women in my family are fierce and outspoken, but never before had I heard of one who was notorious. I set out determined to add flesh and blood to the story of her life and answer the whys in my mind.

What might compel a woman of the 1870s to leave her three young children sleeping in their beds and walk off with a stranger? Why was the husband not mentioned as part of the tale? Where did she go, and how did it work out for her? Who was the handsome drummer who incited her? That whirl of questions propelled me down many a dusty road in Kentucky and through many an hour sequestered and poring over long out-of-print book. For years an image of Lydia sat constantly in the corner of my mind, her long skirt covering legs that were drawn up to her chest, her head resting wearily upon her knees. Often times she lifted her lovely face and gave me a questioning look, waiting for me to tell her story. Finally I could deny her no longer . . .

I WILL START on that chilly November night in 1840 when she was born. It's as good a place as any, but as you will soon discover, the beginning of a story is very hard to nail down and the end is never quite the finishing point.

A LOW THIN cry broke the silence in the chill November air of a small frame house in the backwoods of western Kentucky. Jacob Ross, startled from a dream state, took a few seconds to remember why he was sitting at the kitchen table instead of warm and comfortable on the feather bed with Matilda. Lifting his head, he met the barely opened eyes of his brother William across the table. They listened for a second to make sure the baby's cry was not imagined, exchanged relieved half smiles, and quickly found their feet.

"I'll fetch some more wood. Sounds like we're going to need it." William chuckled as he headed for the front door.

Jacob pulled his grandfather's watch from his vest pocket and noted the time, 6:15. He then went to the stove and started the process of building up the fire that had burned down to coals during the long night. The kettle of water the doctor had told them to boil still simmered on the back burner. It looked like Ma had refilled it during the night.

A draft of frigid air announced William's return. The two men busied themselves getting things ready for the women to cook breakfast, both stealing anxious glances toward the steps as they worked. They turned expectantly as they heard the footfall. The care-worn face of their mother betrayed nothing. "Jacob," she spoke, "It's a girl. She's got all her fingers and toes. Your wife wants to see you." William clapped his brother on the back, stirring him to mobilize his feet.

Jacob took the stairs two at a time, leaving William and Anne Ross alone in the kitchen.

"What is it, Mom?" William asked, seeing a cloud cross her face.

"Is it Matilda? Is she all right?"

In view of William's concern Anne quickly replied, "She is fine, Will. Had a rough time of it, but the doctor says she will be up and about in a few weeks."

"The baby?" William asked.

"Healthy. Pretty little thing too, but . . ." Anne's voice trailed off.

"What are you leaving out, Ma?" Anne hesitated for a long moment before she spoke.

"Oh, it is likely nothing, but I've never seen a new mother react so to a baby. When Dr. Allen handed her to Matilda, she took one look and turned her face away. She said, 'You take her, Ma Ross.' I guess it must be hard, her being all on her own. Did you get any word from Margaret?"

"No, Ma. Ed took the team up there to fetch Matilda's mom as soon as we knew it was her time, but he has not come back yet. He must have spent the night with Margaret and Cornelius after the long ride. I expect we will see them sometime today." They both looked up expectantly when they heard Jacob's slow descent down the stairs. He rounded the corner with a tiny bundle held protectively in his arms.

"Look at her, Will, my beautiful firstborn child. Her name will be Lydia after her great-grandmother." Will pulled back the enfolding blanket to look into the tiny sober face, almost comical in her seriousness. Peeking out of her knitted white cap were wisps of reddish-blonde hair.

"Oh, Jacob, Gram must be looking down from heaven with a smile today. I can just hear Grandpa telling Grandma Lydia she had the temper to match her red hair." William laughed as he recalled staring at Grandma's white hair with a puzzled look and both of his grandparents forgetting their ritual argument and smiling at him. Later Grandma had pulled a little bag out from the bottom of an ancient trunk and laid a twist of auburn hair into his hand.

Jacob followed his brother's thoughts into the treasured memory. "That trunk," he said. They both sank into their own reminiscences. For Jacob it began with the slightly acid, dusty smell of old paper, leather and fabric, then a vision of the sheen of the faded blue satin ribbon that served to hold the lock of hair together. He felt the softness of his grandma's cheek against his as she held him close and told him about being teased for her red hair when she was a girl.

Both he and Will stared again at the tiny new baby and prayed that she would grow up with the same fire and passion as her namesake. The noise of an approaching wagon snapped them from their nostalgia. "I'm as surprised saying this as you must be hearing it, but I hope that's Mrs. Lynn. After all, she is Matilda's mother and I'm certain she will be able to comfort her." He paused and then added, "Matilda is not quite herself, but, well, of course that's to be expected, I'm sure."

Ed came into the room with a valise in hand followed closely by Mrs. Margaret Cox Lynn, unruffled and in charge as always. The volume of her voice was adequate for a grand hall, and it echoed like a gunshot in the tiny cabin. The previously placid baby commenced to wail. All but Mrs. Lynn looked toward the newborn. "Well!", intoned Mrs. Lynn, ignoring the baby's cries. "What are you waiting for, Edward? Sit that bag down and get those horses into the barn." As she spoke, she removed her bonnet and cloak and handed them to the still-befuddled Edward.

He stood for a moment until she gave him a sharp look. With

some difficulty he hung Mrs. Lynn's items on the already-crowded peg beside the door and hurried outside before they fell. She turned her attention to Jacob who was attempting to sooth the newborn. "Let me have that baby and you men go about your business." Reluctantly, Jacob passed the precious bundle to his mother-in-law. "Boy or girl?" she barked.

"A little girl." Jacob beamed with pride.

"Unfortunate," Mrs. Lynn snapped. "It's always better to have a boy first." She stared into the tiny screaming face and gave a disgusted grunt. "And to top it off she's redheaded! I certainly have my work cut out for me with this one. She's going to be a challenge every step of the way."

Although Jacob had only known his mother-in-law for a few years, he had quickly grasped that there was no future in refuting her opinion. Mrs. Cox made no effort to quiet the child. Instead, she turned to the only other woman in the room, Jacob's mother. "Anne," she boomed. "When will breakfast be ready? I've had no more than coffee and a piece of cold bread this morning and have been bounced about on that horrid wagon since before sunrise."

Anne turned from the stove where she had been working for the past half hour and had just popped a tray of biscuits into the oven. There was no affection in the look she gave Margaret. Anyone with eyes could read the exasperation on her harried face, but Margaret, the object of her displeasure, was oblivious. Having been up all night with her daughter-in-law and the doctor, Anne was too exhausted from helping to bring her grandchild into the world even to try for sarcasm. She had known Margaret since they were school-girls and had learned that to say what one really thought around her was even worse than holding one's tongue. With a quick prayer to God for her un-Christian thoughts, Anne replied, "It will be another twenty minutes until the bread is done, Margaret. You can sit and have a cup of tea or go up and visit with your daughter while you wait." She somehow managed a cheerful tone with an only slightly grim smile.

The retreating wail of the baby could be heard up the stairs as Margaret huffed off. "Mother is here. Doctor, you are excused," were the first words out of Margaret's mouth as she entered the room. The good doctor had no compunction to mince words and so replied with scathing derision as he turned to her with a basin containing bloody cloth and the afterbirth.

"So you'll be taking care of this and cleaning up the patient?" Margaret gave him a look that would kill lesser men, but the doctor had already turned away, back to checking to make sure the flow of blood had slowed enough for him to be on to the next emergency.

While Margaret flapped about for something nasty to say, the doctor spoke quietly to Matilda telling her she had done a good job and everything appeared normal so he would be heading off. Matilda thanked him as he picked up the bloody basin and his bag and left the room with not even a nod toward Margaret.

Margaret deposited the still-screaming baby in the crib her son-in-law had so painstakingly made and sat down in the chair beside her daughter. Matilda reached weakly for her hand, and Margaret took it briefly and then patted it with her other hand before letting go. "We have serious issues to discuss about this child," she began. "It is as I feared: a girl and the image of Jacob's grandmother to boot. I have no doubt that she is a bad seed, and we will have to work together diligently to keep her on the straight and narrow."

"Yes, Mama," Matilda replied, "I know, and in spite of all my protests Jacob is determined to name her Lydia after that woman."

A disgusted grumble was Margaret's first reply. "Well, it will serve to keep our goal in mind, to keep our guard up at all times." Baby Lydia's tiny wails increased in volume and urgency. Both women seemed immune to her distress as they continued to plot out her future. Neither of them heard Anne's quiet step as she came into the room, but both fell into a guilty silence as Anne lifted the baby out of the crib and made soothing noises.

"Have you tried feeding her, Matilda?" Anne asked. Matilda looked puzzled. Despite having been the oldest daughter and helping her mother through three births, she looked as if she had somehow forgotten that babies required feeding and comfort.

"No, Mother Ross. I am so exhausted. Could it wait until later?" Anne's sharp look spoke volumes, but her words were carefully even and measured.

"You will both feel better if you let her suckle a bit," she replied as she put the baby in her mother's arms. Anne kept her body between Margaret and her daughter-in-law as she helped guide Matilda to touch the baby's cheek with her nipple. Baby Lydia turned her head frantically and then latched on greedily. The room became silent as the baby calmed and nursed. Anne beamed with love. Margaret harrumphed with spite.

Anne tried for a consolatory tone. "Breakfast is ready, Margaret. Why don't you go down and help yourself? I'll find out what Matilda feels like eating and bring her up a tray."

"No need. I'll bring up a tray for both of us. I know what my daughter likes," Margaret replied with coldness. She huffed out of the room, leaving Anne alone with Matilda and the now-content baby.

"I'll just sit here a bit until you're finished so I can put the baby back in the crib."

"Thank you, Mother Ross, but could you put her back now? It hurts my stomach when she sucks."

"Oh, my dear, I know it's a bit uncomfortable at first, but it will help you get your figure back quickly. You'll see. And of course it's certainly good for the baby." Anne smiled softly as she looked over the peaceful scene, but made no effort to pick up the child. "She's going to be a beauty, Matilda, like her mother. Although the hair is why Jacob insisted on naming her after Grandmother Ross."

Matilda bit her tongue to keep from blurting out her mother's opinion on Jacob's grandmother.

"As long as she is a good Christian girl, I will be happy," Matilda responded, trying to keep her tone neutral. "And of course that she marries a respectable, hardworking man like her father."

Anne smiled and helped Matilda switch the baby to the other breast. They sat in companionable silence while the baby finished and fell off to sleep. Anne was thinking of gathering her up to put her in the cradle as Margaret stormed into the room dictating instructions to her son-in-law who followed with a tray. Jacob deposited the tray on the first empty surface, the corner of the washstand, and then stood in an uncomfortable silence trying to decide what to do next. The baby whimpered at the noise, and seeing Jacob's hands free, Anne gathered sleepy baby Lydia from her the new mother's arms and passed her off to her son.

"You want to take her downstairs Jacob so Matilda can get some rest after she eats?" Anne asked. Jacob smiled proudly and took the baby out of the room with Anne close behind. "Let me know when you finish and I'll come get the tray," Anne said as she left the room.

THE NEXT FEW weeks were a torment to everyone in the family. Margaret, far from being a help to her daughter, treated everyone as if they were her servants. Both the baby and the new mother cried most of the night and often in the day. Jacob gave up on trying to appease his weepy wife and scolding mother-in-law and took to sleeping on a pallet he made on the floor of the cold front parlor. Well-meaning neighbors dropped by at odd hours with homemade pies and contradictory advice. Jacob's mother, Anne, plus his brothers, William and Edward, took turns riding over from their neighboring farms to help with chores until Matilda was back on her feet.

In mid-December they awoke to find a light skim of snow on the ground. Jacob came in from the morning milking with exhaustion written on his face. Matilda was up trying to clean up the kitchen while her mother sat complaining in the rocking chair and the baby screamed upstairs. "Mother Lynn," Jacob announced, "Get your bag packed. I am taking you back home today before we get more snow."

Margaret gave him her steeliest glare. "I'm sure Matilda will have something to say about that!" They both turned to look at the exhausted new mother. Matilda paused briefly and observed her dog-tired husband and sour-faced mother as if seeing for the first time.

"Oh, Mother dear," she exclaimed, "how selfish I've been. Papa must miss you so terribly. Jacob, why did you let me keep Mother here with the weather coming? I'll go right up and pack for you. Just stay right there. Jacob, come help me, please."

Margaret sat abashed as they hurried up the steps. She thought she heard a sound like a muffled giggle, but it might have only been Jacob clearing his throat or the final protest note from the now-silent infant, Lydia. Jacob returned twenty minutes later carrying her valise, followed by Matilda holding little Lydia. Jacob set the bag on the floor and went to the wall peg for Margaret's coat.

"Am I to go off without even a bite of food?" Margaret huffed. Quickly Matilda laid Lydia in the cradle Jacob had made and wrapped the remains of last night's corn pone in a towel, then handed it to her mother as she kissed her on the cheek.

"You will never know how much these past few weeks have meant to me, Mother. Have a safe trip home and give Father my love." Matilda gave Jacob a quick secret smile as he picked up the valise.

When Jacob returned, it was almost dark, but the mules knew their way home. He unhitched, wiped them down, and saw to their feed by lantern light. "Thanks, old boys," he said. "You're a good team." He saw that William and Ed had been over to do chores for him and noted that he owed them something special for the past few weeks. Heading for the house, he saw a flickering light in the window and hoped his bride was still awake. The door opened just as he approached, and the warmth of her arms welcomed him home.

The next morning the soft whimper of the baby woke him at first light. Matilda was up and nursing her before he realized that it was the first time since Lydia's birth that they had spent a quiet night. "She slept through?" he asked. Matilda nodded and smiled.

A deep sense of contentment settled over Jacob. His patience had been tested these past few weeks, but he and Matilda had weathered the storm. He felt his heart swell with emotion, love for his wife and the new precious child, gratitude for family and friends to help in times of need, and a good crop that was all safely gathered in for winter. He even spent a few moments trying to be thankful for his sharp-tongued mother-in-law. All he could manage without hypocrisy was that she bore the beautiful woman by his side, the mother of his child. Softly he touched the tiny head of his daughter and looked into her bright, clear eyes. "I hope you are half the woman your great-grandmother was, Lydia. You have a lot to live up to."

Matilda's heart froze. She knew she should censure her words, but emotion and her mother's constant criticism for the past few weeks poured out of her mouth. "I let you name her Jacob, but do not think it's because I admired your abolitionist grandmother. It was to remind me I need to work hard to make sure she does not turn out like that woman." Jacob's heart sank. His grandmother was a guiding light in his life, a smart, strong, intense woman who had earned the respect and admiration of most everyone who knew her.

"Those are your mother's words, Matilda, not yours." Jacob swung his legs out of the bed, pulled on his clothes, and left to start chores. His tone had a finality that Matilda knew to leave alone, but the grim set of her mouth as she looked down at the baby was easy to read. Her duty was clear. If she could not count on Jacob to help her, she would shape and mold this child alone.

GRADUALLY THE RHYTHM of life on the farm took on its familiar pattern. The less busy winter months gave Matilda and Jacob time to adjust to a baby in the house. Matilda did complain that Lydia was always hungry and demanding, and she seemed to resent the time spent feeding and caring for her. Of course, with little experience being responsible for a little one, Matilda had no idea how fortunate she was to have a happy healthy child who ate greedily, fell asleep peacefully, and only rarely woke her in the night. Matilda gained a new admiration for her husband who never seemed to tire of helping out with Lydia. Many mornings she found him down in the kitchen with the stove already warm, cradling the wee one in his arms, while Matilda got some much-needed sleep.

Christmas brought the nearby family in, but since Matilda's mother-in-law had been there so recently, she stayed home close with her other grown children. Jacob cut sweet-smelling cedar branches to brighten the mantel, and Matilda made mince pies using the jars she had put up in the summer and stored in the root cellar. William's wife brought a ham from the pig they had slaughtered and smoked last year, and Ed contributed a roasted turkey he had shot and dressed earlier in the week. Everyone dug into their stores for winter vegetables to roast or boil. Great-uncle Jesse had come over early with surprises, store-bought presents, and a basket of expensive treats to share: oranges, nuts, peppermint sticks, and coffee. Christmas morning Matilda put together a triple batch of biscuits, and everyone sat down in warm companionship to enjoy the feast.

The afternoon was spent carelessly, as if it would last forever, a luxury for a busy farming family. As shadows outside lengthened, there was a brief pause in the chatter and laughter. William took the opportunity to stand and announce, "Well, as much as I hate to say it, my animals are not taking a holiday. I think it's time to head home."

Jesse looked down at the angelic face of his tiny grandniece, who was looking so intently into his eyes as he held her, and wondered why this child spoke so to his heart. Perhaps it was the unwillingness he sensed in Matilda to fully embrace her firstborn daughter. Maybe it was because he felt his mother's spirit moving behind the clear eyes and serious, unblinking stare of the baby.

"William's right, Lydia," Great-uncle Jesse said, addressing his grandniece, "but you can be sure I'll be back every chance I get." Jesse made a silent vow in that moment to protect this child as long as he lived. Lydia whimpered for a few seconds as he handed her back to her mother. Everyone bundled up and headed to their homes, Ed rode with William and his wife, Ginny, to the house across the creek they built when the brothers were both bachelors. Great-uncle Jesse set off in his buggy to the nearby family home that had been built by the man he called his father.

After years of profitable travel Jesse had returned to Kentucky and shared the house with his mother after her husband died. With his wealth he was able to add on to the simple cabin, purchase comfortable furnishings, and fill his mother's last days with contentment and happiness. He rarely spoke of his early life to the rest of the family, but there was always an undercurrent of sorrow in him that spoke of some past tragedy. Lydia's birth seemed to have stirred some old memory that brought him both pain and joy.

ONE NIGHT IN EARLY FEBRUARY, while the sky was still pitch-black, Matilda woke with an urgent need to use the chamber pot. Tucking back into the warm bed afterward, she had almost fallen back asleep when the realization came to her that she had been feeling a little unwell lately, with a lot of the same symptoms she'd had when she was first expecting Lydia. The thought refused to be pushed out of her head no matter how hard she tried to tell herself that nursing mothers did not get pregnant and it was normal not to have a cycle for some time after having a baby. Finally she fell back into a fitful sleep and woke with a start when she heard a voice, clear as a bell, say, "So are the girls twins?" It took some time to realize she was all alone in the room and to shake off the scary message of the hallucinatory voice.

Jacob was his usual cheerful self when she got downstairs, but reading his wife's mood, he made every effort to lighten her spirit. She remained distraught throughout the day. That night when he tried to gather her in his arms, she stiffened and seemed repelled by his touch. Jacob did not press her but lay there puzzled. Both he and Matilda had been quite innocent when they married, but quickly the intimate part of their life had become a source of joy and delight. He had been surprised when she was the one to initiate lovemaking after Lydia was born, in fact on the very night her mother had finally left them on their own. There were the occasional nights when both of them were too tired for anything but sleep, but they still reached for each other and dozed off entangled. Ever-patient Jacob just patted his troubled wife on the back for a minute and said softly, "Good night, Mattie. Sleep well." Hearing only silence, he rolled over and sank into a fitful sleep.

SPRING CAME SUDDENLY to the rolling farmland of western Kentucky that year. Redbuds bloomed in welcome surprise on the ridgeline above the farm, and the night was filled with the insect-like noise of tree frogs awakened from their winter sleep. Jacob finished the monotonous morning chores of feeding and milking the cows, giving mash to the horses and slop to the pigs. He headed back into the house for breakfast and chuckled to see Lydia chewing on her toes in the cradle. She gave him a gummy smile when he bent over to tickle her chin. Matilda had just put plates of eggs, sausage, and cornbread on the table and sat in her usual place. Jacob knew something had been on her mind for weeks, but each time he tried to press her, she turned away. This morning he saw a shift in her as she caught his eyes and looked at him directly. He waited patiently for her to speak.

"Jacob," Matilda said, louder than was necessary, "I have to tell you something." Jacob's mind raced with a dozen possible disastrous announcements his wife might make. Finally she spoke, almost too softly for him to hear. "I think I have another baby in me. I fear it might be a second girl." Jacob jumped up to embrace her, splashing his coffee across the table.

"What wonderful news, Mattie!" he exclaimed. "Why did you not tell me sooner?" He pulled her close into his arms laughing in relief that none of his fears were realized. "Did you think that I would not welcome another baby, no matter if it might be a girl?"

Matilda had tears in her eyes now. "But, Jacob, it's so soon after Lydia. I just . . . I . . . ."

"I have to go tell William and Ed!" Matilda seemed genuinely surprised at Jacob's joy as she watched him shovel breakfast into his mouth like he was starving. As soon as he was done, he took a minute to talk to the ever-interested baby Lydia. "You are going to have a sister, Lydia, or maybe a brother. Isn't that exciting!" Such was her father's animation that Lydia not only smiled, she let out her first real laugh. Jacob put a kiss on each of her plump little cheeks and headed for the door.

MATILDA BECAME MORE and more anxious as her belly swelled through the spring. Her nights were restless, and mornings came early. Lydia seemed to be thriving, but Jacob was concerned about what Matilda would do with two little ones both wanting to nurse. Margaret, Matilda's mother, had not been feeling well for some time now and could not travel. Because her presence had been so little help during Matilda's last confinement, it was a relief not to have to ask her to come. Jacob gave it a lot of thought and finally spoke to Uncle Jesse.

It was mid-June when Jesse showed up one day in his carriage with a snip of a girl seated beside him. Matilda was hanging laundry when they arrived. The child wore a threadbare smock and pinafore, her thin stringy hair braided, her expression sad. Jacob came out to greet them with his usual hearty welcome. "Morning, Uncle Jess! Wonderful to see you! And who have we here?" he asked, nodding to the girl, who squirmed in discomfort and would not meet his eye.

"This is Abby. She's come to help Matilda with Lydia and the new baby." Jesse stepped out of the carriage and helped Abby down. He walked over and picked up a sleeping Lydia from the laundry basket and handed her to the strange girl. Matilda started to protest, but Jesse interrupted, "Abby, why don't you take Lydia inside the house and get acquainted?" As they walked away, Matilda noticed that Abby's face took on a happy expression as she talked to Lydia and she seemed to know exactly how to hold and comfort her. Matilda turned to Jesse and Jacob as she watched them walk into the house.

"What is going on? Where did you find that child, and why did you bring her here?"

"It was me," Jacob said. "I asked Jesse to find me someone to help you out. You know you're exhausted now, and when the new baby comes, it's going to be worse. I have too much to do with the crops and the animals to be of much use to you. Please don't be upset, Matilda."

Jesse spoke up. "Abby is the second girl in a family of eight. She has helped her mother since she could walk, so she knows babies. Her parents are struggling to feed them all. I am paying her family her wages, and I'll give you money for her food. You'd be doing her and her family a favor Matilda, and she is just staying until school starts in the fall." Matilda's silence dragged out for an awkwardly long moment while the men stood waiting for her to speak.

"Well, if it's done, I'll just have to deal with it, won't I?" Matilda's words did not match the look of reprieve on her face.

Jacob breathed a sigh of relief and gave his wife a hug. Jesse, reading the conflicting emotions from Matilda, pondered briefly on the state of his nephew's marriage, then said, "I'll be heading home, folks." He climbed back into his rig and raised his voice to a slightly higher pitch. "Gee up!" he said, and the wagon rolled away down the dusty road.

Matilda grumbled and went back to the laundry, but after supper was over, with the house in order, she and Jacob lay together under her the quilt she and her mother made together before her wedding. She reached her hand over to touch her husband's shoulder. "Thank you, Jacob," was all she needed to say. He put his strong arm around her and pulled her close.

"So glad you're happy, sweetheart," Jacob said.

Matilda went off to sleep with a feeling of contentment she had not felt since Lydia was born.

TWO

THE BIRTHDAY GIRL

LYDIA LAY in bed for a few minutes with her eyes closed after she woke anticipating the excitement of her long-awaited eighth birthday. It was still dark outside, but the overeager bantam rooster demanded the sun to rise at his command. Soon there would be the noise of people stirring about the house, but for these few minutes Lydia could be alone with her dreams. Great-uncle Jesse had promised her a surprise, so she let her mind wander with delicious anticipation about what it might be. She wondered if her mother would make a special dinner like she did for her brother Jake when he turned seven in August.

Quietly, so as not to wake grumbly Jake or her other dear little brother, Josiah, Lydia washed her face, dressed, and made her bed. She tiptoed down the steps into the dark kitchen and headed to the outhouse while the rest of the family slept. The cool morning made the usual stench a bit more bearable as she sat down to relieve herself. She washed her hands in the ice cold water bucket on the porch and went inside. Her dad came down the stairs just as she closed the door.

"Well, if it isn't my little Lydia all bright eyed and bushy tailed this morning. Wonder why she's up so early?" Lydia giggled with delight as her dad scooped her up in his arms for a hug.

"It's my birthday, Pa!" Lydia giggled again and kissed her daddy's scratchy cheek.

"Oh my!" Papa responded with a fake tone of surprise. "If that's the case, we better get done with chores so we can celebrate. I'm heading out to the barn. Why don't you come with me and help me feed the animals?" Lydia nodded her enthusiasm, happy to do anything to please her father. Taking three steps for every one of his, she scurried to the barn, picked up a bucket, and began to fill it with corn for the chickens. After they were all out in the yard, she slipped into the henhouse to steal eggs from their still-warm nests. She was ever so careful as she put them in the straw-lined basket, but just as she was picking up the last one, the old rooster entered the house and flew up at her in a rage. Terrified as she was of the rooster's sharp claws and beak, Lydia protected the filled basket by wrapping both arms around it. In doing so she lost her grip on the one egg she was holding, and it landed with a splat on the wooden planks of the henhouse floor.

"Mean old thing! Look what you made me do," Lydia yelled at the rooster and shooed him away as she headed back out the door, holding carefully onto the egg basket.

By the time she got back to the house, Mother was bustling about the kitchen. "Good morning, Mother. I fed the chicken and gathered the eggs. There are thirty-three of them today. There would have been thirty-four if the mean old rooster hadn't made me drop one." Lydia was proud of her math skills, which she had learned from her Uncle Jesse. Because of him she was ahead of all the other students her age in the local school, even though she had only started going a year ago.

Lydia's mother's sharp tone brought her back to reality.

Her mother stood with hands on hips and mouth tight as she

hissed, "You are a wicked child to blame the rooster for your care-lessness. Shame on you!"

Lydia hung her head. "I'm sorry, Mother. It was my fault. I know the rooster is just trying to protect the hens."

Barely appeased, Matilda gave orders as she turned back to her work. "Put those eggs away, and mind you don't break any more. I'll need to use every one of them today."

A tiny bit of hope soared in Lydia's heart. Mother was going to make her a cake! She was sure of it, but she dared not ask. She did as she was told and then hurried about helping her mother with breakfast chores. She set the cups, plates, spoons, and forks around for Papa, Mama, Uncle Will, little Jake, and herself, then filled the porridge bowl for baby Josiah so it would have time to cool. Mama finished cooking eggs just before Papa and Uncle Will burst through the door. Jake climbed up to the table, and Lydia hurried to help her baby brother into his chair as Mother put the biscuits in front of Papa's place.

"You forgot the jam, Lydia," said Mama accusingly. Lydia rushed to the cupboard to get a fresh jar of the wonderful blackberry jam her mother had made from the summer's bounty.

As they all settled in at the table, Papa put a heaping spoonful of jam on her plate. "A special helping for my best blackberry picker," he announced. Lydia glanced up and saw her mother's silent disap-proval etched in the lines around her mouth.

"Oh, Papa," Lydia pointed out, "I just picked them. Mama's the one who did all the work of making the jam. You made it taste like summer in a jar, Mama."

Papa put jam on Jake's and Josiah's plates too. Jake ate his immediately, not bothering to even put it on his bread. Josiah, in his usual serious fashion, took tiny nibbles first of bread, then of jam. Lydia laughed at the differences in her brothers: irascible Jake who wanted everything to happen now and Josiah, a little old man in the body of a four-year-old. Papa's eyes twinkled as he and Lydia silently shared their observation of their divergent personalities, but Mama scolded Lydia.

"Stop making fun of your brothers!" raged Matilda, even though Lydia had not said a word. Lydia's good mood collapsed on her face, but Papa came to her rescue silencing Mama with a look and a quick, "That's enough, Mattie. Lydia is just laughing along with me."

Josiah, hearing Pa's rare sharp tone, froze midbite and started crying. Jake, oblivious to the conversation at the table, continued to stuff his mouth full of biscuit, salt pork, and eggs. Mama scooped up Josiah and went upstairs, with Papa following in her angry wake. Jake quickly spooned all of Josiah's jam into his own mouth, then readied himself to go outside quickly.

Lydia sat terrified trying to think of a way to fix things. She could hear the irate voice of her mother and the urgent whispered response of her Papa. She could not clearly make out what they were saying, but it was so familiar by now, she knew the script—her mother convinced Lydia was the devil's own child and Papa vainly trying to prove her innocent. Uncle Will, who had sat impervious to this familiar family squabble, gobbled down his food, gave Lydia a kiss on the cheek, and left without saying a word. Lydia watched him retreat back to the yard through blurry eyes. Lydia did not expect him to take her side over another adult, even though she suspected he sometimes wanted to. With appetite gone she went to draw more water to wash up the kitchen.

Papa found her at the well and helped her get the bucket up without spilling too much. "Lydia," he said softly as he lifted her chin. "You did nothing wrong. Your mother is having a rough time lately what with the two babies and losing her mother so recently. I know you always want to help her, but let's both try especially hard to keep the peace."

Lydia gave her Papa a look that she hoped did not betray her guilt at not feeling any sadness at her grandmother's September burial. Having lost her beloved Grandmother Anne in the spring had made the contrast of her feelings for the two sides of her family sharp in her mind.

"I will, Papa." Lydia looked into her Papa's sad eyes and vowed to make more of an effort to be good. She paused recalling how much she missed the quiet, gentle presence of Abby. Until she was five, she did not realize the hired girl was not her sister. Ma treated her the same, making her defer to the boys, ordering her to do chores along with Lydia. She looked up longingly at her Pa. "I just wish Abby could come back."

"We all miss her, Lydia. She stayed with us much longer than she intended, but now she has a home and a husband. We need to be happy for her."

Lydia sighed. "I am, Papa, honest I am. I'm just sad." Knowing it did no good to linger over things that she could not change, Lydia went on with a resolve that she hoped sounded more sincere than she actually felt. "I'll do all my chores and help with Jake and Josiah and read my Bible verses every day, just like you and Mama tell me. I promise, Papa."

"That's my good girl, Lydia." Papa sounded hopeful, but his eyes didn't look any happier. Slumping under the weight of the water bucket, she headed back to the kitchen hoping her mother's wrath had subsided.

It did seem as if the air was cleared, and the rest of the morning went a little better. The noon meal time came and went without any major clashes, and Lydia began to hope again. Washing up the last of the dishes, she said, "Mama, is Uncle Jesse coming to supper this evening?" Since her grandfathers had passed right after Lydia was born and her great-uncle had no children of his own, Jesse was the grandfather of her heart. Despite the differences in age and experience, the two seemed to share one soul. Jesse had spent long years collecting a treasure trove of books. Lydia had spent many a happy Sunday afternoon listening to him read stories of dragons, kings, explorers, and heroes. Lydia had begun to read them for herself since she turned five, starting with the few picture book primers and moving on to nursery rhymes, then more serious books. The ever-patient Jesse helped her with harder words and encouraged her to think beyond this little corner of the world.

Mother's expression darkened. "No! Why would I want that crazy old man here?" Lydia's heart sank. As Jesse's interest in her had grown, Mother's opinion of him had diminished. She saw Mother's mouth grow tight, her shoulders square. She braced herself, eyes on the ground, for the next blow of hands or words. Long seconds passed with no sound or movement. Finally curiosity overcame her fear, and Lydia raised her head. For a fleeting moment she saw something in her mother's eyes, a softening, a flicker of maternal doubt. "Take Josiah outside and make sure to keep a close eye on him. Take care Jake isn't worrying the chickens or playing in the horse trough while you're out there."

"Come on, Josiah," Lydia chirped with an enthusiasm she did not feel. "Let's go see if we can spot any wild turkey from up on the ridge." The sturdy little boy followed after her with obvious excite-ment. The hundred-odd acres of the Ross farm were all the world they knew. Their house was set on a flat rise of a rolling hill looking out over the split where Crooked Creek divided its waters unequally. The wider portion bordered the fertile fields where Papa and Uncle Will grew corn and sorghum, the trickle of the smaller stream twisted around the other side of the ridge.

Jake soon spotted Lydia and Josiah climbing the hill and joined them. Lydia made up a song for her brothers along the way. All Lydia's songs featured her brothers as the heroes of some adventure, a dragon slayer or a brave soldier. Lydia shushed them, and they grew quiet as they reached the top. They crept through the under-growth near the edge of the old growth timber to the place where the forest floor was uncluttered and still. All three flopped down on their bellies and looked down to observe. The glint of the sun showed the track of the stream of water down below. Most of the trees had shed their load of leaves, allowing trails of light to filter down in spots. Lydia breathed in the mossy damp smell of the ground, and they watched a fat chipmunk stuffing acorn in his jaws. Josiah let a confused fuzzy caterpillar walk over his hand, causing them all to giggle.

Jake's patience gave out quickly. "Make the noise, Lydia," he demanded in a failed attempt at a stage whisper.

Lydia smiled and tried her best to do the turkey yelp call her father had taught her, then paused and listened. They all lay still for a long minute before Lydia tried again. "It's not working, Lydia," Jake said. "Do it right!"

Suddenly Jake jumped up. An unearthly sound came from his mouth that might have been his version of the turkey call. It wasn't so much a yelp as a yell, jagged and loud enough to startle every animal in the territory.

"Jake!" Lydia said sharply as she watched the retreating squirrels and birds. "You scared them all away. We might as well go on back to the house. We sure won't see a turkey today."

Jake wailed in earnest, "I'm gonna tell Ma!" Josiah and Lydia got up quickly to follow Jake's retreat down the hill. Josiah stumbled through the thicket of underbrush as he tried to run too. Lydia rushed to help him and took her eyes off Jake who was running down the hill yelling, "I'm gonna tell!" over and over. Looking back instead of where he was going, Jake stumbled and fell. Being on a hillside, he started to roll on the gradual embankment screaming like he was being stung by hornets. Lydia scooped up the considerable weight of Josiah and headed after him as quickly as possible while keeping her little brother safe. She had almost reached Jake as he stopped on the level where the cabin stood. At that moment the back door swung open, and out came Mama.

"Mama, Mama!" Jake screamed, standing up and rushing to bury his face in her skirts.

"You wicked girl," Ma said, giving Lydia a look that spoke murder and snatching Josiah from her arms. "Go straight up to your room. I will deal with you later."

"But, Mama . . ." Lydia's voice trembled. "I didn't do anything. Jake . . ."

"Don't talk back to me, Lydia. Go!" Lydia saw the look of satisfaction on Jake's face.

Upstairs in the room she shared with her brothers, Lydia sobbed quietly into her pillow as she entertained murderous thoughts: her mama thrown from a runaway horse, her hands reaching up as she drowned in the creek's fast waters, a scream as she was attacked by a wild panther in the woods. After a time the terror of what she was thinking washed over her, and she began to pray not to be left a motherless child. By the time her mother came up the stairs, she was contrite, not for anything she had done but for the uncontrolled workings of her clearly evil mind. When Mama opened the door, Lydia rushed forward and fell to her knees. "Oh, Mama, I'm so sorry. Please forgive me. I love you, Mama."

Matilda Ross was taken aback. She was feeling a twinge of remorse for her treatment of her firstborn on her birthday and had been willing to give her the benefit of the doubt. With Lydia's reaction of obvious guilt, she reconsidered. Jacob would be upset with her, but she didn't care. This child would be the death of her, always scheming, always trying to look like the innocent in front of Jacob.

"I'm going to give you plenty of time to think about what you did while you help me with the laundry. Go fetch water so I can start it heating, then set up the wash tub outside."

Lydia scurried to do as her mama asked, trying hard not to spill too much from the heavy bucket. She set up the washtub on the wide front porch and collected dirty clothes, soap, and the washboard while the water heated. Her mother came out with the kettle of boiling water and added it to the washtub. Lydia started with the lighter clothing and soon got into the rhythm of scrubbing, wringing out, and putting the washed items aside. The sun was almost at its zenith when she finished. She looked up and saw her pa and Uncle Will headed to the house for dinner. Pa patted her head fondly, and then he and Uncle Will picked up the washtub and took it to the garden to empty. Lydia was already at the well pulling up more buckets of rinse water when they finished.

"Come on, Lydia," Pa said. "You must be hungry after all that work. Let's go eat."

Lydia emptied the clean water into the tub, added the soapy laundry, and gratefully followed the men into the house, her stomach rumbling. Ma barked orders to everyone in general but did not single Lydia out with her sharp tongue. Lydia felt the ache inside her let up a bit and even dared to hope the rest of the day would be better.

They ate a good meal of cornbread, beans cooked with ham, and stewed dried apples on the side. The conversation around the table was about the livestock and the plans for next spring, easy comfortable talk like it usually was with Papa there. As soon as she finished, Lydia began collecting the dishes and putting away leftover food. It was nap time for Josiah, and Mama took him to his bed as he protested he was not tired. Lydia washed the dishes and listened to the chatter upstairs. It soon grew quiet, and Ma came back down the steps as Lydia finished the cleanup.

"I have to get busy finishing that laundry," Ma said. "It needs to be hung up so it can dry before nightfall. I need you to watch Jake while I get it on the line."

When Lydia had put away the last dry dish, she headed outside where Jake had collected sticks to make a pretend village. Lydia walked about finding more sticks and pebbles for Jake to use. With Jake happily occupied Lydia made a few more trips to the well to help Mama fill the rinse tub a second time. Mama worked quickly to ring everything out and carried the clean clothes to the line. Bloodthirsty Jake had built cabins and a teepee in his village and was in the process of making a line of soldiers to attack. Since he was content, Lydia went to the clothesline so she could hand Mama the clean clothes a piece at a time. Even though it was cool, the sun was bright and warm on her back. Her mind daydreamed about birthday surprises, but she didn't dare hope for too much.

Mama's voice brought her back to reality. "Lydia, finish hanging these clothes. I need to go check on Josiah." Mama had hung all the big pieces so Lydia could make quick work with the shirts and socks. Suddenly Lydia was startled by a male voice.

"Well, if it isn't my busy little ladybug Lydia!"

"Uncle Jesse! You scared me," Lydia gasped. She ran to him and hugged him tightly. Uncle Jesse beamed and held out a little brown paper-wrapped parcel toward her.

"Happy Birthday, Ladybug," Jesse said softly. "I hope you like it."

She quickly tore the brown paper off the package. Inside was a wonderful book. It had pictures on every page, and it was written in both English and Latin. Her delight was quickly replaced with a realization.

"Oh, Uncle Jesse, I love it, but . . ." She turned to make sure her ma was out of earshot. "I need to make sure it's okay with Mama."

Jesse's face was sad, but he reassured her that he understood. "I'll keep it at my house, but it's your book. You may come and read it anytime. How about tomorrow? Can you get away Sunday afternoon?"

Lydia's eyes brightened, and her feet danced a few little steps of excitement. "I really, really hope so, Uncle Jesse. I'll be good as gold until tomorrow, and I think Mama will let me come." Then she remembered supper and hung her head. "I'm sorry you won't be here tonight." Immediately she perked up again. "But I am so glad I got to see you today. Thank you so much, Uncle Jesse!"

Jesse took her chapped little hand in his and gave it a kiss. "You're welcome, Ladybug. I'm so proud of you. You look more like your grandmother every day, so beautiful." He tucked a stray strand of her auburn hair that had fallen out of her bonnet behind her ear and headed back toward the woods where he had tied his horse. "See you tomorrow." Lydia watched him until he was out of sight and then hung the last few pieces of laundry. Picking up the empty basket, Lydia hurried back to the house with a hopeful spring in her step.

It took her eyes a few minutes to adjust to the dark interior of the house after being so long in the bright sunlight. She took off her bonnet and hung it on one of the low pegs beside the door. Mama was sitting quietly in the rocking chair, eyes closed. Lydia could hear the boys chattering upstairs, so she headed up to keep them quiet so her ma could sleep a bit longer. Josiah exploded with shrieks of joy when he saw her. The noise gave Jake license to start wailing. She heard Ma's angry voice from downstairs, "Lydia Ross! Stop it this instant!" Lydia sighed. Why did Ma always think the worst of her, and how did she even know she was upstairs? Jake, hearing his mama downstairs, headed for the steps.

All the way down he yelled, "Ma, Ma," at the top of his lungs. Lydia shook her head. She could not understand why Jake was so hostile to her. Josiah's chubby little arms clung around her neck when she picked him up and walked softly with him down the steps. Right before the last turn she heard Jake and Ma whispering conspiratorially. Lydia could not quite make it all out, but she heard "Your sister has the devil in her," so she knew it was not good.

Lydia swallowed the hard lump in her throat and stomped her feet up and down on the step she was standing on trying to make it sound like she was just coming down from the top of the stairs. When she walked into the kitchen, Ma and Jake were both looking at her with the same disapproving expression. Lydia forced a smile onto her face and asked Ma what she could do to help with supper. The moment passed, but the words carved another tiny cut in her heart next to so many others that had scarred over but still ached.

Supper was not the celebration she had hoped for, but it was not as bad as it could have been. They ate the two rabbits Pa had caught in a snare that morning, fried up in bacon grease and served with gravy and biscuits. Ma had made a persimmon pudding for dessert, not Lydia's favorite, but since sweets were rare, Lydia and the rest of the family praised Ma for serving such a treat.

After the table was cleared, Lydia hurried to gather the dry clothing off the line before the sun went down. The basketful was admittedly a bit haphazard, but she would smooth them out later inside after nightfall. She carried the laundry into the house and placed it behind the pantry curtain. Ma was getting the little ones down for the night, and Pa was sitting by the fire smoking his pipe and looking pensive. "Papa," Lydia asked softly, "was I good at supper? I felt like Ma was angry with me. Everything I say seems to go wrong."

"My sweet girl," Papa replied, "I see how hard you try. You know Mama is having a rough time, but she loves you very much. Just be patient a bit longer, pumpkin. She'll come around. Now go get ready for bed. The Lord's day tomorrow but the chores will still need doing."

"Just one more thing, Papa. Can I go see Uncle Jesse tomorrow afternoon after all my work is done?"

"I'll make sure you get to go. Now off to sleep with you." Lydia's heart was full. She washed her face and hands, got into her nightdress, and lay down on her narrow bed. For a long time she tried to keep her eyes open as she silently mouthed the only prayer she knew, the morbid one that ended with, "If I should die before I wake, I pray the Lord my soul to take." She then added, "And bless Ma and Pa and Jake and Josiah and Uncle Jesse and Uncle Will and Uncle Ed."

Lydia lay awake wondering if God even had time to listen to little girls. Lydia doubted that he did with all the other important people in the world vying for his attention. With her tangled eight-year-old logic Lydia tried to figure out what she did wrong today. She had felt such excitement this morning when she had heard the mean old rooster outside demanding the sun rise at half dawn. Still, she rationalized, it could have been worse. At least she had gotten through the day without a spanking. Lydia lay in the darkness and tried to count her blessings, not the smallest of which was a trip to Uncle Jesse's tomorrow. She slipped off to sleep before she ran out of things to count.

THREE

FAMILY SECRETS

THE FIRST PINK-AND-GOLD light of morning fell across Lydia's narrow bed, filling her with joyful anticipation. Life always seemed better at dawn with an unblemished day stretching ahead. It was Sunday, but the circuit preacher was not scheduled this week and Papa had promised her a free afternoon with Uncle Jesse. Over the past three years since her eighth birthday Lydia had slipped off to visit with him at every opportunity, rushing through her chores so she could spend more time reading and talking to him. It was easier now that Jake and Josiah were older and Ma seemed to have calmed down a little.

Lydia sprang out of bed with anticipation, dressed, and headed downstairs to help her mother with breakfast and then to the barn to check on the animals and her father. The rest of the morning was spent working with Ma to get dinner ready for the aunts, uncles, and cousins who were due to arrive around noon. She was old enough to be equal to her mother in the kitchen and almost equal to her father in completing most of the farm chores. The new table her papa had recently made was groaning with food: roasted venison, slices of ham, fried chicken, baked root vegetables, tiny new potatoes with peas, wild greens cooked with salt pork, fresh stewed rhubarb, and hot rolls made with white flour and wild yeast, a rare but welcome treat. To top it off, there were five kinds of pie and a butterscotch cake sitting in the cupboard ready for dessert later that afternoon, although Lydia could not imagine how anyone would still be hungry.

The conversation around the dinner table was on the same boring topics as always, crops, new livestock, and family members who had long passed. During a brief silence Lydia decided to ask a question. She immediately regretted speaking as most everyone at the table turned to stare at her, and Ma's look could have frozen the water in the creek. Clearly, she had said something that was taboo, but she had no idea what that might be. The conversation had been about dead relatives, so what was wrong with asking about her great-grandmother? Lydia wished she knew, but clearly it would have to wait until she could talk to Uncle Jesse. Uncle Will picked that moment to reach for another of Ma's rolls, but the basket was empty. "Lydia!" Mom said sharply, her eyes pointing to the basket. Lydia repressed the urge to mention that Will had already eaten five as she hurried back to the stove to load it with hot fresh bread.

Conversation had changed back to other topics by the time she got back to the table. She passed the basket down the row and listened to the men rehash the same old tired subjects they talked about every month when the family got together. She knew she would not be able to slip away until after dessert was served and she had washed and dried the last of the dishes. When the meal was finally done, Lydia asked permission from her father to head to Jesse's farm. While his yes was still sitting in his mouth, she grabbed her coat from the hook and threw open the front door in one motion. She was out of the yard and down the path before Ma could get out a word of objection.

Even if Ma had yelled, she would not be heard over her new puppy Belle's whoops of joy at having her favorite human to join her in a romp. Lydia's long legs made short work of the miles between home and Jesse's farm. Belle circled around her looking for game to scare in the brush, but always keeping in sight of Lydia. They arrived at Jesse's doorstep with ticks and burrs clinging to them both, the ties on Lydia's braids lost, and her auburn hair hopelessly tangled.

Jesse had been sitting on the front porch rocker anticipating her arrival. He greeted Lydia and Belle with enthusiasm and laughed as he watched Lydia sit down and start pulling burrs off Belle's short coat. "Ladybug, looks like you picked up a few burrs too." Lydia looked at her woolen stockings and sighed. "Get those off before you come inside," Jesse said as he rose slowly out of the rocking chair. Lydia picked most of the larger objects off her stockings, left her shoes outside the door, and then headed down the dark foyer of the house to the library where Jesse would be waiting. Belle scrambled off to romp for a bit until his human came out of the house again.

Lydia followed the familiar steps down the hall to her uncle's library with its book-lined shelves, heavy mahogany furniture, and velvet drapes. Jesse was already settled down at his rolltop writing desk, so Lydia took the familiar green wing chair beside him. "So what are we investigating today, Ladybug?" Uncle Jesse looked at her from over the top of his glasses. Lydia thought for a while trying to find a way to ask a question about family secrets. Jesse smiled as he watched her pick her words carefully, the way he had taught her. Lydia finally decided to be direct.

"Secrets, Uncle Jesse. I need to know why everyone at my house never wants to speak about my great-grandmother, Lydia, and why they get angry with me if I ask about her." Lydia paused and turned through her mental store of "dictionary words" that Uncle Jesse had insisted she learn, until finally she came up with one she felt would work. "Was she notorious?"

Uncle Jesse chuckled and patted her hand. "Oh, my sweet girl.

Yes, well, perhaps, or at least some might call her that, but I think we could find some better words to describe her. You have heard bits and pieces from me, but let me tell you the whole story from beginning to end, and you can decide for yourself. You are certainly old enough to understand. It starts in old Virginia around 1780. I was just your age when we set off, and my brother Silas was around seven, but much of the trip is still as clear to me as if it happened yesterday. We camped on the ground many nights until the wagons made it to Pittsburgh. I had never slept in the open before, and I remember struggling to shut my eyes the first night because a panther was screaming and the horses were restless. My father sat up with his gun for half the night and then turned it over to Burwell, the slave who was traveling with us.

"At the time I did not realize how unusual it was for a black man to be trusted with a gun. Pappy and your great-grandmother were inordinately kind to Burwell and his wife. Pappy's father had given the slaves to him in his will, but he never believed in slavery. Pappy gave Burwell a choice to come on the trip to Kentucky and made promises to him that he would be a free man with land when we got there.

"Burwell was unusually smart, and although uneducated, he had learned to read and do math while sitting and watching Pappy do his schoolwork. Pappy often let him read books he owned, although it was forbidden for slaves to be educated at the time in old Virginia. I remember him helping build the raft that would float us down the great Ohio River. Burwell had an instinct for figuring things out and made a lot of suggestions that your great-grandmother later wished we had followed. Pappy would have, but the other men who were at Redstone Fort building rafts for their families began to mutter among themselves against Pappy and his 'slave-loving' ways. Pappy decided just to go along with the majority on the raft building, reasoning that it had worked for most of the other travelers going out west. Once complete, we rolled wagons onto the raft, carried or drove the rest of the livestock on board, and headed a few miles down the Monongahela River toward the Ohio. Being too late in the season to start downstream, we tied up along the banks with thirty or so other rafts and prepared to wait for spring.

"I don't remember ever being as cold as I was that winter. Chunks of ice that broke up in the Allegheny regularly floated down the Ohio and crashed into each other all day and night. That along with the wolves howling in the distance and the occasional panther scream soon became background noises for our dreams. I learned to live by the rhythm of the river, the misty fog of fall morning, the cold quiet of the short winter days, and the birdsong that was especially beautiful as the spring days grew warmer.

"One morning I woke early and lay half asleep, cocooned in my warm blankets. It was unusually quiet, just the occasional splash of a fish trying for breakfast. Panthers and wolves had long finished their hunting and were off sleeping in their dens. Sound travels on the water, and I heard an unusual mummer of voices. When I slipped out of my cozy nest and dressed, I saw Pappy standing and chatting with the other men gathered around the fire in the half dawn. I drew closer and listened.

"'I'll take the lead raft, being single and having floated rivers before,' said the man everyone called Dutch. He was a giant of a man, but despite his bearlike exterior he was gentle with all the children in the makeshift camp and always had time to play games and cut up with us. He was traveling with his two younger brothers and the brides they had taken right before they left Pennsylvania. Rumor had it his intended wife had balked at the last minute, fearful of the rigors of the trip and of never seeing her family again. He was younger than my Pappy by ten years or so, but his bearing inspired confidence in the others, and they listened when he spoke. Excited, I ran all the way back to our tent to wake my mother and tell her we were finally starting west again.

"The next few days were spent packing our goods back onto the flatboats. They seemed to have multiplied twofold in the months we had spent camping on the south bank of the river. We all slept on the boat that last night in late March to be ready to set out at sunrise. When morning arrived, Mother wanted Silas and me to stay with her under the boat's awning for safety, but Pappy felt I was old enough to help out on deck. Through most of our first weeks our pattern was the same. Ma, Silas, and Burwell's wife, Lettie, mostly kept busy fishing, repairing clothing, preparing the game the men had hunted the night before, getting meals ready, and making leather goods we would need in the wilderness. Pappy, Burwell, and I worked to keep the flatboat in the center channel and avoid sand-bars, snags, and rocks.

"My part was mostly staying in the front of the boat, keeping an eye on the leaders ahead of us and shouting out 'Right' or 'Left' to the men. After the long months of building the boat and then waiting on the bank for ice to melt, it was exciting to move so swiftly in the spring rush of water. Every mile took us deeper into Indian territory, and it became the job of all the youngsters to keep a sharp outlook for any activity along the banks.

"The boats were all halted and tied up late in the afternoon, giving the men time to do some hunting for dinner. A boy from the head of the group told me he thought he had seen an Indian in the woods earlier that day, but the men on the boat did not believe him. He was a fanciful youngster, and no one else saw any Indian sight-ings that day. We were still greenhorns and likely overlooked the signs.

"As we boys helped the women get ready to make the evening meal, we suddenly heard terrified shouts of 'Indians!' echo through the woods, soon followed by the reappearance of affrighted men running as quickly as they could through the tangled underbrush. Everyone rushed to grab the small amount of gear we had carried up the banks and retreated to the relative safety of the boats. I kept looking for Pappy and Burwell to come out of the woods, and finally I spotted them, Burwell's arm holding Pappy up and an arrow protruding from Pappy's chest, plus one in Burwell's other arm. They were followed by Dutch holding both his and Pappy's guns. I ran in their direction, and Dutch shouted to me to take Pappy's gun, and he would be the lookout while everyone else got on the boats.

"Minutes stretched out like hours until we got everyone back on board and launched again as the sun dipped low in the sky. Dutch came on board with us to get the boat moving. We traveled on down the Ohio for another hour or so until it got too dark to see at all. We came to what looked like a somewhat safe harbor in the gathering gloom. Ma and Lettie worked on Pappy, removing the arrow and trying to stop the flow of blood. The arrow in Burwell's arm was removed last after they got Pappy settled down with some whiskey in him for the pain.

"After Lettie seared the wound with a knife heated in the fire, Burwell silently clamped his teeth down into a leather belt and kept his screams inside for fear of attracting any other natives in the area. I will never forget how Dutch treated me during this time, expecting me to take on a man's work without any question in his mind that I was capable of doing so. It's what got me thought the next few days while Pappy weakened and finally breathed his last.

"Four days later we buried Pappy on a bluff above the river, disguising his resting place to protect it from desecration from wild animals or Indians. Dutch put his arm around me briefly and then around Ma and Silas for longer. He spoke to her about his last conversation with Pappy, who asked Dutch to look out for us if he didn't make it. The next weeks on the boat were very hard for all of us, especially my mother. She kept up a brave face during the day, but I could hear her sobbing quietly in her bed at night.

"The river flows one way and there is no turning back, nor is there time for a long grieving period in the wilderness. While we all missed Pappy desperately, Dutch made life bearable, filling in our empty spaces like the missing piece of a puzzle. During the next two weeks what was left of my childhood slipped away unheeded into the murky water of the broad Ohio. When we reached landfall at Limestone, we were an odd sort of family. No one questioned we would move on to our claim as a group.

"By the time we had hauled all of our goods overland to our property on Sun Creek and gotten a shelter built, Ma and Dutch were functioning as parents. Dutch's brother's claim was less than a day's ride from us, but after visiting once and seeing that they were doing well, he picked up some of his tools, blankets, and clothing and came back to help us finish clearing and planting a small plot we hoped would get us through the winter.

"I was old enough to figure out what was developing between him and Ma. At first after Pa died, she had leaned a lot on me, talking over her worries about the future and sometimes crying because she missed him so much. One day many weeks after Dutch started staying at our claim, I heard a welcome sound, my mother's laugh. I had not realized how much I had missed the ring of laughter. It made me remember the happy times back in Virginia where someone was always cutting up.

"It was late August when Dutch and I were out harvesting the corn crop that he spoke to me. 'Jesse,' he said, 'I need to ask you how you would feel if I were to marry your mother?' It came as no shock to me at that point because I had seen they were getting closer as they talked around the table at the end of each day. I know I might have resented most any man stepping into my father's place, but not Dutch. He was already friend and family. I could not imagine life without his strong, steady presence.

"There were no preachers in those parts at that time, but the settlers within a few days' ride of us came together in late September for a meeting and celebration of our survival. It was held over at Dutch's brother's claim with three other groups from nearby. Dutch and Lydia made the announcement of their intent, and there

were immediate cheers and good wishes from the group. They
spoke some simple vows and agreed they would stand in front of
the next preacher who visited the area and make it legal.

"That winter Dutch moved his sleeping spot from in front of the
fireplace to behind the curtain with Mama. A circuit rider came by
in April and said some words over them, and in June the next year
my sister Sarah was born, named after Dutch's mother. It's the way
things went back when Kentucky was mostly wilderness. No one
ever looked at Sarah differently except for your mother's people.
Sarah was a beauty like you, Lydia, auburn hair, skin like cream,
and like you, she was no frail flower. She was outspoken and opin-
ionated like her mother, with the confidence of a warrior. That did
not stop her from being courted by a number of the eligible men
around the area when she came of age, including your grandfather,
Cornelius. That certainly got your grandmother Margaret's nose out
of joint."

Lydia laughed at this point trying to imagine her rigid Grandmother Margaret mad about her boyfriend hovering around the
beautiful and bold young Sarah. "Where is Sarah now, Uncle Jesse?
I've never met her, have I?"

Jesse's smile was bittersweet. "No, Lydia, she met her match
when a young calvary officer came through the area. He was handsome, ambitious, and confident in his charm. He spotted Sarah at a
Christmas party she attended with a distant cousin she was visiting
in Bardstown. She was floating down the stairs in a pink dress, and
he was struck dumb by her beauty and grace. The look on his face
and the uniform he wore would have been enough to make any girl
at the party swoon, but not Sarah. Although only seventeen and a
country girl who should have been in over her head, she was clearly
not impressed. The young captain was flabbergasted when she
ignored him. He ended up resigning his commission and marrying
her two years later.

"She left a number of broken hearts on the shelf on her wedding day, including your grandfather Cornelius. Sarah and her husband headed off to California in 1824. He soon established himself as a trader and became quite wealthy. I get a letter from time to time. I think she's happy, but I will always miss her.

"There is another part to this story, and it might be the real reason your mama gets riled up about your great-grandmother. She kept the promise my pappy made to Burwell and Lettie. She let them build their own place about two miles from Dutch and your gran, but none of the ground for either farm would have been cleared nor crops planted if not for his and Lettie's effort. Mom gave them freedom papers that she had carried with her from Kentucky, and before she died, she deeded them the forty acres they and their growing family had cleared and worked. Now, with all this stirring across the country about slavery and people taking sides for and against, it has caused a lot of anger, divided so many families. Your dad's grandmother seems to have landed on one side of that disagreement and your mom's family on the other.

"When I was a child, Burwell's son Ralph and I played together as friends. We worshiped together, prayed to the same God, and even if his skin was darker than mine, we both bled red when we were cut. Dutch and my ma taught me to look for a man's deeds first, and that's what I read in the Bible too."

Lydia had been uncharacteristically quiet during Jesse's telling of the story. Now he sat silent, waiting for her response. After some long minutes Lydia began, "I see a lot of dark-skinned people when we go to buy goods at Miller's place. Some of them scare me, but most of them seem to be just trying to get by, like we are. Once there was a girl around my age with a pretty lavender calico dress and the sweetest smile. I stopped to talk to her when Mama wasn't looking. She was nice, and I would have liked for her to be my friend. Then Mama spotted me and came running like I was being attacked by a wild dog. She grabbed me by the arm and dragged me away, telling me never to talk to one of those again. I tried to get her to explain why, but her answer made no sense."

"Do you understand any better now, Lydia?"

"No, Uncle Jesse, I don't really think I do. There are bad people and there are good people, dark-skinned people and light-skinned people. I think it's the way they act that makes them good or bad, not their skin."

Jesse smiled and regarded this child of his heart. She harbored no evil or unkindness in her. His only fear for her would be that she might assume that others were like her, without malice. "Tell me, Lydia," Jesse spoke earnestly, "if you could have any life you wanted, what would you choose?"

On this subject she did not have to think. In one breath Lydia said, "I want to travel to those far places I read about in your books. I want to be able to go to a university and learn about science and math and literature. I want to learn Latin and Greek and French and all the other languages so I can talk to everyone I meet. And after I have visited all those places and learned all those things, I want to write a book about what I've seen and done so other girls will know that being able to cook and clean and have babies is not the only thing women can do."

"Great plans indeed, my dear. How about we start working on your ideas today?"

"How can I do that, Uncle Jesse? In school we only study sums, reading, and writing. Ma and Pa already think I know enough and want me to stay home next year and help out on the farm."

Jesse hid his concern. "I will speak to your pa, Lydia. I will make sure you continue here in school until you are at least seventeen, and I will also tutor you every week. I can help you with some science and geography. We may need someone else to help with languages as mine have gotten rusty after all the years of disuse. One other thing," Jesse said as he opened the lower drawer of his desk and pulled out a bound journal. "I want you to start writing every day. It will be a beginning for that book of yours."

"But, Uncle Jesse, I have nothing to say. My life is sooo boring!"

"You must look closer, my dear. So much is going on around you that is much more interesting than you realize. Just start writing it down. You will find your voice as you put the words on paper. You do not have to share any of it with me unless you want to, but I would love to hear how it's going from time to time. When you fill this one up, I will give you another. Plus I promise, if you apply yourself to study, I will make a path for you to find your dreams. Girls are not encouraged to obtain higher education now, but times are changing. In fact, I have a book for you written by a woman who is shaking things up." He reached into his desk drawer and pulled out a slim volume entitled *Woman in the Nineteenth Century* by Margaret Fuller. Lydia held it close and resisted the urge to start reading immediately.

"In many cities like Chicago and maybe even Louisville," Jesse continued, cheering her on, "there may soon be schools for you. My beloved wife and I were never blessed with children, Lydia, but if we had been, I could not have wished for one more perfect than you."

Time always passed so quickly in the glow of Uncle Jesse's encouragement. Lydia heard Belle whooping outside the door and realized she was long overdue home. She jumped up and hugged Uncle Jesse and tried to thank him, but how do you thank a genie who promises to make your dreams come true? She would have to hide the book under her mattress and read it in secret, but read it she would.

FOUR

NO FRIGATE LIKE A BOOK

LYDIA'S BRAIN was simmering with a heady blend of excitement, dread, and confusion. She had skipped and run halfway down the road to her first day of school term this morning until she realized that she was now an upper-class student and should act the part. She then let Josiah and Jake run on ahead while she practiced pretending to be mature and worldly-wise, no small feat for a thirteen-year-old country girl who had never been more than twenty miles from Ohio County. Still, as Uncle Jacob often quoted, "There is no frigate like a book to take you worlds away." The tomes in his library had indeed taken her around the world and back again. It was clear to Lydia, from the lecture she had heard this morning, that her mother did not approve of those foreign ideas. "Don't be trying to show off all that stuff you read this summer, Lydia. No one likes a know-it-all. Just be quiet and do what you're told, and do not correct the teacher!" Lydia bit her lip like Uncle Jesse did when he was worried.

Of all the faraway places she read about, the one volume that had changed her the most was the short tome from Margaret Fuller that let her explore the inside of her own brain. Did anyone else ever give woman's lot in life any thought at all? She knew her mouth was so often ahead of her good sense, but she would try to keep her revolutionary thoughts to herself. After all, there was a brand-new school teacher for her class this year, a woman! On top of it all, there was Albert McGee, a boy two years older, handsome, arrogant, and usually indifferent toward her, but other times pinning his focus so narrowly on her that she felt like a bird trapped in a thornbush. She was pretty sure she hated him.

She heard the school bell ringing and realized she had slowed her pace too much while fantasizing about the day ahead. She began to run, and when she finally burst into the school door flushed, thoughts jumbled and bonnet half off her head, she crashed directly into the brick wall that was Albert McGee. "Well, if it isn't Lady Lydia, the pride of Ohio County," Albert boomed with sarcasm. Lydia felt the heat rising in her face as she looked up at the rawboned boy blocking her path. Before she could open her mouth to vent her irritation, she heard a cross female voice from the front of the room.

"Children!! Quiet! You are late. Hang your things and be seated!" The voice came from a woman who did not look much older than the ninth grade girls in the class. Her pinched mouth and fiery eyes made it clear she was irritated. Lydia rushed to follow instructions and find her seat at the back of the room beside her classmate Beth. Albert grinned at the pretty blonde teacher and took his time finding his place across the aisle. Lydia was astonished to see the teacher try to stop herself from smiling back at Albert. To hide her inappropriate emotions, she turned, wrote "Miss Porter" on the chalkboard, and said, "I will expect each of you to answer to your names as I call roll."

As she began, Lydia finally looked around the room. There were mostly the familiar faces of the children she had known since she was a baby, but there was one new boy. He was blond, perhaps a year younger, with a soft, kind face, almost cherubic. All thoughts of Albert McGee evaporated as Lydia waited patiently for Miss Porter to call his name. She reached the end of the roll and then looked up one last time.

"Anyone whose name I did not call?" The new boy raised his hand tentatively. "Oh yes, Duncan," she said. "Of course." While she had called everyone else's last name, Duncan's remained a mystery, one that Lydia had to solve before the day was over.

Miss Porter spent the morning placing the students into appropriate groups. Despite their age difference Albert and Duncan were called up to the higher-level math group along with two other older boys, herself, and her seatmate, Beth. The math material Miss Porter presented them with was difficult, but Lydia was able to figure it out fairly quickly. Albert did it easily, as did Duncan. When the advanced reading group was pulled, several of the other girls joined, but the boys were not included except for Duncan and Albert. At reading time it was clear that Albert was not especially interested in the book they passed around to read aloud. Lydia became so wrapped up in the Charles Dickens novel, she was slightly crestfallen when Miss Porter announced lunchtime. By the time she walked to the back of the room to fetch her lunch pail, all thoughts of Dickens had been superseded in her mind by her curiosity about the mysterious and handsome Duncan.

The other girls were already outside on the grass huddled close to eat and gossip. Lydia did not have an intimate friend in the clique and normally would have tuned out their gossip. But today she pulled her best friend, Beth, close to the margin of the circle so she could listen.

"And she and her brother are rooming with Ada Finch!" stage-whispered Nancy Young. "You know she has that big house and no family anymore. Miss Porter is her second cousin once removed." Nancy kept talking and gesturing broadly until the whole story was dramatized. There was a general murmur from the group with the agreement being that a number of the girls had set their cap for

Duncan, but none more intently than Rachel Renfrow. Lydia had to concede that Rachel was pretty enough, but her sharp tongue was the very thing that kept Lydia from wanting to be part of their inner circle.

She sat digesting the information that Nancy announced about Duncan. Imagine, Miss Porter was his sister! The rest of their family had been killed on the Ohio River right before they reached Kentucky. Lydia was not certain about the part of the story where Duncan heroically rescued his sister from drowning but was unable to save his mother, father, or the youngest brother. Miss Porter was determined to take care of her brother, but since all they owned had sunk with their boat, she did not have the funds to return east. A stroke of luck and connections with another of the party traveling with them landed her the teaching position in the same neighborhood with her distant relative Ada Finch, who was an ancient widow whose children had long left for adventures further west.

Lydia glanced across the yard to the group of boys who had already wolfed down their meals and were organizing a game of some sort. It was impossible to tell what the rules of their sport might be, but Lydia suspected they made them up as they went along. She saw Albert talking to Duncan and trying to pull him into whatever they were playing. She wondered if he knew about Duncan; then she immediately realized that gossiping Nancy lived the next farm over from Ada Finch, and Albert's and Nancy's mothers were close. Mrs. McGee was not one for idle chitchat, but she was as curious as the next person in their small, closed community. It was a harmless bit of news that would be difficult to keep contained. With his eye always on the main chance, it was no wonder that Albert would cozy up to the teacher's brother.

The girls had started picking the long-stemmed clover flowers from the nearby field and tying them together to make garlands to wear around their necks, heads, and wrists. Lydia watched jealousy as the boys ran about the yard with abandon, laughing gleefully. She longed to join them as she had when she was younger and like she did with her brothers at home. She refused to understand why there were so many things that girls could not do since they always seemed to be the fun things. Mother said it was not "ladylike" to run about so, and Papa said he was fearful she might get hurt because she was so small. It was easier to accept Papa's version, except there in the schoolyard were eleven-year-old Jake and eight-year-old Josiah playing along with boys who were almost grown men. She often asked Uncle Jesse why some things were women's work and some were only meant for men. Jesse was very progressive, and while he believed women were as smart as men—"Maybe smarter," he always added with a wink—she still did not think even he could ever see them as equals.

The clang of the school bell interrupted Lydia's daydreaming. When she looked up, she noticed that the boys had stopped playing and Albert and Duncan were standing close together talking. Both seemed to be looking directly at her. Lydia's face flushed pink, and she kept her head down as she trailed into the building with the other students. Afternoon classes were a torture because each time she looked up, at least one pair of eyes were on her. It would be either Albert with his bold gaze, a shy look from Duncan, who then pretended he was staring out the window, or the burning, jealous scrutiny of Rachel Renfrow, who had quickly grasped that she had competition.

When Miss Porter dismissed school, Lydia was the first up from her seat and flying out the door. She only slowed when she heard Josiah's little voice calling for her to wait up. He was full of news of his day, retelling everything as if Lydia had not been sitting in the same small room with him. Still she listened to every word and encouraged him, even agreeing to help him with his letters when they got home. Of course, when they arrived, Ma had other plans for both of them. Josiah went with Jake to the barn to help Pa with chores while Lydia was set to chopping onions and potatoes, gathering wood and water, and getting the table ready for supper. Ma worked beside her mixing up bread and stirring the skillet and pots on the stove.

When Pa and the boys came in, Pa said grace, and then Ma and Lydia set the food on the table. Ma had made Papa's favorite hash with the leftover boiled beef from Sunday's dinner, frying it up in saved bacon grease with the onions and potatoes Lydia had chopped. A pot of fresh green beans that had been seasoned with ham scraps had simmered since morning on the back of the stove, and hot cornbread fresh from the oven rounded out the meal. The table was silent for some time as everyone enjoyed the bounty.

Finally Pa spoke up asking each child in turn about their school day. Josiah went first because he was youngest and about to burst with news. "Miss Porter is the bestest, prettiest teacher ever!" he exclaimed. "I like her sooo much more than old Mr. Stanley we had last year." Lydia, Pa, and Ma all smiled. "Old" Mr. Stanley was all of twenty-five and had moved on to apprentice at a law firm in Leitchfield. Lydia had liked him well enough, but she had to admit that Miss Porter had a lighter touch with the young ones.

Josiah, being the third child, would talk as long as he had a listening audience. Finally Pa finally cut him off gently and moved on to Jake. "And what did you think about Miss Porter, Jake?"

"She's okay," was his two-word critique. Then he went on with much greater enthusiasm. "The older boys let me play with them today! Albert says I have a great arm. There's a new boy called Duncan who helped me up to the first branch so I could climb the big tree in the yard. It was so much fun! I went almost to the top before the teacher rang for us to come back inside. Duncan and Albert even waited to make sure I got down okay, but I never needed any help." At this point Pa interrupted what was quickly becoming one of Jake's well-known big brags.

"Do you have homework, Jake?"

"No sir," Jake replied. Pa looked at Lydia for confirmation.

"Miss Porter just told everyone to practice anything that seemed hard for them today. She told the little ones to copy their letters and numbers but did not assign anything special to Jake. I'm sure that will change tomorrow."

"What about you, Lydia, how did you like the new teacher?" Ma asked, surprising Lydia with her seeming interest.

"She was fascinating. She held everyone's interest, and the older boys minded her. I know you told me we had a female teacher this year, but did you know she and her brother are orphans and he was going to be joining our class?" Lydia asked.

"Yes, I did, but I thought it best to let you meet her and make up your own mind. She has had an unfortunate life," Ma said, as if it were somehow Miss Porter's fault her parents were dead.

"I think I'm going to like her a lot," Lydia said. "She had us reading Dickins and gave us some math work that was more of a challenge than any Mr. Stanley had given us. Both she and her brother seem like they are very smart and determined people."

Unhappy that he was no longer getting attention, Josiah piped up. "Duncan said you were the prettiest girl he ever saw. He and Albert talked about you all during lunchtime." All eyes turned to Lydia, who blushed a deep pink for the third time that day. She felt Ma's eyes on her, so she rose quickly from her chair and started collecting dishes to wash.

"Get your slate, Josiah, and we'll practice those letters as soon as the table is clear." Lydia's voice sounded a little too high and strained.

Pa smiled gently, but Ma's mouth looked like she had tasted something sour.

A few weeks later on a Friday morning Lydia woke in the predawn hours with a sick, cramping feeling in her lower stomach and a headache. As she slipped out of the warm bed, she was over-taken by a wave of nausea. Heading quietly down the steps, she grabbed a shawl to wrap around her shoulders as she headed out the door to the outhouse. Looking down as she slipped bare feet into her boots, she saw a spot of red staining her white nightdress. She glanced around her guiltily to make sure no one else was about. She pulled the gown hastily over her head, then slipped off her bloomers and dropped them both into the bucket of water on the back porch. Picking up the bucket, she headed down the well-worn path to the outhouse. Out of sight, she cleaned up as best she could with an old towel that had been hanging to dry on the porch. Squatting down, she rinsed and scrubbed as much of the blood as she could out of her clothing and hung them to dry on the fence just out of sight of the house. All the while, she contemplated what she must have done to make this happen.

It was true that of late she had been putting exploring hands where her mother told her not to touch. That had to be what caused the bleeding down there, Lydia conjectured, but how to stop it? There was no one to tell of her wickedness. Her thin body shivered as she walked back to the house, head down in shame, clad only in her undershirt and the oversize shawl. If only she could get back into the house without anyone seeing her. She opened the door as quietly as possible and saw no light, but just as she closed it softly behind her, she heard the strike of the lucifer. She gasped as Mama turned around with the lighted match and saw her there in her undressed state.

"Lord ha' mercy, Lydia. You scared me out of my skin." Mama took in the scene in a split second, turned and lit the lamp with the match, and then walked over to Lydia. "Where are your nightclothes?"

Knowing she was likely to be punished regardless of what she said, she decided to go with the truth. "Hanging on the back fence. I . . . I . . . they were . . . there was blood . . . I washed them out in the bucket."

Much to Lydia's surprise, Mama's face softened. Eyes downcast, she walked over to the cupboard and pulled out a stack of folded pieces of white cloth, which had been hidden in the very back, and a clean pair of drawers. She showed Lydia how to position the cloth and make it stay in place with special fastenings.

"Go upstairs and put this on, get dressed, and then come back down. We'll take care of the gown on the fence and have a little talk later."

Mama was kinder than usual when Lydia came back down, but she gave very little explanation.

She did not seem startled that blood had started gushing from her daughter's private parts, but Lydia did not for a minute think this could be normal. What she could not understand was Ma not being angry with her. "Go get dressed for school now, Lydia," Ma said.

Lydia headed up the steps with a heavy heart, her insides still feeling like they were being squeezed by demons. Between the pain and the confusion, the tears she had been holding back were now streaming down her face. Solemn-faced Josiah came into her room and patted his sister on the arm. At only seven years old Josiah showed signs of being a budding champion for justice. Although he was just a little boy, he could see that their mother treated Lydia more harshly than she did either Jake or himself, and he idolized his older sister. "It's okay, Lydia," Josiah said softly. Lydia suppressed a sob, gave Josiah a quick hug, and lay down on her narrow bed.

Ma called up the stairs, "Come down for breakfast, Lydia. You'll be late getting to school."

Still sick and miserable, Lydia rose and dressed. Before she went downstairs, she looked to see if she was still bleeding. "Ma," she called down the steps, "I'm not hungry and I don't feel well. I don't think I can make it to school today." In a few minutes she heard her mother's footsteps on the stairs.

"You can stay home from school today, Lydia, but you must go on Monday. You will feel better then but . . ." Ma searched to find words while Lydia waited to discover what her punishment was going to be for whatever she had done. "You are a woman now, Lydia. As your body adjusts, I expect it will be less painful. It is for me now."

Shocked and incredulous, Lydia exclaimed, "This happens to you too? Is it some family plague?"

Ma actually laughed. After the boys were gone, she took an hour off from chores, and for the first time ever she and Lydia talked, woman to woman. Later, when Lydia recalled that conversation, her most enduring memory was her mother's warnings about boys. It was a confusing conversation as Lydia tried to determine which boys her mother included in the warning. Her pa? Her brothers? Uncle Jesse? Her mother's exasperation grew at Lydia's seeming inability to grasp her meaning. Her final definitive statement was, "I mean the boys in your class, Lydia, especially strange ones like Duncan. Never let yourself be alone with a strange boy. They could try to take advantage."

"What about Albert, Ma? Would he try to . . ."

"For goodness' sake, Lydia, no. You've known Albert your entire life. We know his parents. He would never try to shame you." For the life of her Lydia could not figure out exactly what her mother might mean. She thought about Duncan's kind and gentle demeanor contrasted with Albert's endless teasing and pushing. She would feel much safer alone with Duncan.

For some months afterward Ma treated her differently, like she was almost an equal, but by the time spring came, it seemed the novelty of her newly realized womanhood had worn thin. Pa came in one Sunday morning seeing Lydia dressed in her best church dress with her white pinafore tied around her tiny waist. "My goodness, what happened to my little girl?" he exclaimed. "You grow more beautiful every day, Lydia." After that morning Ma started treating Lydia even less like a daughter. Some things she did and said reminded Lydia of Rachel Renfrow's snide remarks and looks.

One day, after a particularly unkind comment, it dawned on her that her mother somehow considered her a rival.

What Lydia needed most during this time was a friend. Her mother had never encouraged her to form friendships with girls her age. In fact, Mama had no close female friends either, which puzzled Lydia even more once she and Beth became close. Beth was a godsend when she went back to school on the Monday after her unexpected bloody Friday. Lydia had been too embarrassed to talk about why she had missed class, but when she went to Miss Porter at lunch to do makeup work, the teacher smiled knowingly at Lydia's reluctance to talk. Had she guessed? Did her newfound womanhood show?

Lydia was horrified and wondered if she had been the last one to know about this rite of passage. When she sat down to eat her lunch near the girls, dear sweet Beth leaned near and whispered to her, "Why were you out on Friday?" When Lydia blushed and stammered, Beth put her at ease. "Remember when I was out of school for two days and then missed church? I had gotten my monthlies for the first time. I was thinking maybe it was your turn. Mama let me stay home, and then the weekend came. I have so many questions. Can you come to my house after school tomorrow and we can talk?"

Lydia was too stunned to speak but shook her head affirmatively. It had been a long time since she had visited with Beth. She hoped her ma would let her go. She decided to ask at supper that night in front of Pa. Success! He said yes before Ma was able to protest. Ma gave him a disapproving look and complained, "I need Lydia to help with chores after school."

"She is getting older now, Mattie. She needs to have time with girls her age. Beth will be a good influence." Pa's statement was delivered lovingly but forcefully. Ma had nothing else to say at the table, but later that night she heard her name mentioned in the conversation that floated up the stairs. She could not make out exactly what was said, but it seemed like Pa was defending her.

Lydia's heart was light when she walked home from Beth's the next afternoon. She never realized she could have so much in common with a girl she had just been casual friends with all these years. Beth's ambition matched Lydia's concerning school and visiting faraway places. The difference was that Beth's family encouraged her goals. In spite of Beth saying she had many questions about her "lady business," it was Beth who was able to fill her in on the facts, especially the part about being careful around strange boys. Beth had two older brothers who were protective of her and gave her some facts about the male perspective on sex. Between the brothers and growing up on a farm, Beth had pretty much figured out what men and women did when they were alone together.

By the time they had concluded talking, Lydia did not think she would ever blush again, but it was good to feel less guilt about her body and to learn that the stirrings of desire she had been feeling were normal. Lydia's musings as she dozed off that night were about how wonderful it would be to have a sister like Beth and to live in a family like hers. The next morning she did not exactly recall her dreams, but she woke with a longing she had not felt before. It was not her normal intellectual yearning but an actual physical ache akin to hunger or thirst. Her hand went to the forbidden place between her legs briefly before Josiah threw open her door, bursting with some bit of childish news that would not wait. She rose to dress and start the day while listening attentively to his latest discovery.

Hers could wait.

FIVE

A WOMAN IN THE NINETEENTH CENTURY

THE ANGRY CHOP of the hoe against the hard-packed soil rang like gunshots in the still morning air. The steady rhythm of Lydia's arms stopped briefly while she leaned down to pull another large rock from the garden plot. Removing her stiff starched sunbonnet, she drew back her arm and launched the rock expertly into the growing pile of small boulders she had uncovered this morning. Straightening her back, she leaned briefly on the hoe to view her handiwork. A disappointingly small portion of the large rectangle was exposed black soil, compared to the vast green expanse still ahead.

Despite the cool of the spring day her mouth tasted of salt from the steady rivets of sweat that streamed down her face. Her loose cotton dress clung to her damp body, revealing the growing swell of breasts and hips. Her form felt unfamiliar to her as she ran her hands across her bosom, her waist. Getting her flow was dramatic, but she really was not paying attention to the rest. It seemed as if one day she was a child straight as a beanpole and the next a woman with full hips, chest, and a bothersome, persistent longing of body and soul.

Suddenly she heard her mother's voice, sharp with an edge of something familiar she could not define but recognized as dangerous. "Lydia! Get that bonnet back on your head! Your skin will be as dark as one of the field hands."

Lydia quickly lifted her bonnet back over her auburn braids and mouthed a hollow apology in the petulant tone that had characterized all conversations with her mother in the past year. Mama continued her critique of Lydia's appearance, her attitude, and her lack of accomplishment. She avoided saying anything about seeing Lydia touching her body a few minutes earlier. As Ma twisted the unspoken reproach into acceptable Christian conversation, Lydia daydreamed.

"Lydia!" came the sharp exclamation. Mama had learned long ago how much more damage she could do with a word than with a blow. "Are you listening to me?"

"No ma'am, I'm sorry. I was thinking about church tomorrow," Lydia lied. "It's been three weeks since Brother Stewart has been here. Are you sure he's coming Sunday?"

Mama's voice softened marginally but did not entirely let go of the wrenching feeling the girl elicited in her. Nothing about their relationship had ever been comfortable, but the past few years had become worse for them both. It took all of Lydia's considerable skill to stay on her mother's good side. As for her ma she knew she was being played but did not or would not speak honestly with the daughter whom she had always considered a thorn in her side.

"Yes, Lydia, he's already here, staying with the McGees. Duncan Porter came by this morning with the news and those squash seeds Ada Finch promised me last fall. Of course, we will never get them planted unless you quit lazing about and get this ground ready, young lady."

Lydia heard nothing her mother said after Duncan Porter. Albert McGee had staked his claim for her as his girlfriend last year with little regard for her feelings, but it was Duncan who occupied her dreams waking and sleeping. Since both of the handsome boys sought out her company, most of the other girls in the class kept her at arm's length, except for Beth. Lydia and Beth often talked about boys, but more often their conversations were about visits they would take to big cities someday. Lydia knew her parents wanted her to forget travel and school and settle down with Albert because his family was prosperous and well thought of in the community. Lydia's thinking was that after she finished college, she and Duncan would settle down in some big city. Her parents pointed out Duncan was an orphan with no prospects for the future, but he was the opposite of Albert in all the ways that were important to Lydia. Albert was blunt, bossy, and took himself too seriously while Duncan was kind, picked his words carefully, and was able to laugh at himself.

A tumbled, confused picture rose in her mind when she thought of the two. She had known Albert since the day he pulled her pigtails on the first day of school ten years ago. She did not share that long history with Duncan, but she felt a kinship from the minute he arrived at school two years ago. Albert's broad shoulders and his determination that she was already his were both frustrating and appealing.

She recalled that day last year when she had impulsively joined in the boys' games by throwing a snowball that hit Albert in the back of the head, much harder than she intended. Her target had been her brother Josiah, but Albert had stepped into the path of her swing at the last second. She remembered his angry blue eyes as he charged at her, fierce as a wild animal. He stopped inches from her unwavering, unapologetic green eyes, his fists clenched. He looked as if he wanted to hit her, but instead just stood there with a contorted look on his face. After a few long, tense moments he turned on his heels and left without a word. Since that day Albert began a strategy of going out of his way to ignore her, but somehow she was never able to spend a quiet minute talking to Duncan without Albert suddenly appearing.

She had heard the girls gossip about Albert. He had a quality of danger about him that they foolishly seemed to favor. He was admittedly handsome, tall with broad shoulders, icy blue eyes and thick black hair, but if truth be told, she favored the less flamboyant Duncan whose clear gray eyes looked directly into hers when she spoke, making her feel like she was the most beautiful girl in the world.

She tried to assume a disinterested pose as she waited for her mother to stop talking. "Is Duncan still at the house?" Lydia asked, trying to sound casual.

"Now, why would he hang around? You think he came to see you?" Mama did not try to hold in her laughter. She even seemed to find Lydia's hateful glare amusing.

"Why would I care?" Lydia lied. "I set no store by him. I just wanted to make sure he's gone before I come home for dinner."

Mama's smile was unreadable as she lifted a package concealed in her apron and handed it to Lydia. "Well, you'll surely be safe by then. Here's something to tide you over until the dinner bell rings, Miss Persnickety." Lydia took the proffered sack, gave her mother a begrudging smile and thank-you, and then watched as Mama's long, quick strides propelled her back over the ridge.

Laying down the hoe, Lydia pulled open the drawstring of the calico bag. Inside was a cold biscuit and some salt pork left from this morning's breakfast and a tin cup to dip into the spring. She took a bite as she walked down the hollow toward the artesian well. Say what you will about Mama's temper, her biscuits were the best in the county. Even cold, they were delicious, with a crisp crunch on the outside, then a pillowy, buttery softness within. As hard as she tried, Lydia's were never quite as good.

The artesian well was a quiet, mossy oasis in all seasons, a place where time seemed to stand still. Sheltered in a grove of trees and bounded by the larger brothers of the limestone boulders she picked endlessly out of the garden, it had a peaceful feel about it. Lydia often escaped here on hot summer days when her brothers were off tending the cows or the cornfields. The boys frolicked naked in the water when they came back from their chores in the summer, but as bold as she was, she had never had the nerve to try bathing there.

Tonight after supper was done, she would have a turn in the galvanized washtub set up in front of the woodstove in the kitchen, the lye soap Mama made from wood ash and lard turning her skin bright red. She thought how wonderful it would be to jump into this clear, clean pool instead or to have a real tub like the Egyptian queens, right inside the house. She thought how grand it would be to have servants fawning over her as she flopped down unladylike on her belly to reach the source of the fresh bubbling water.

The crack of a twig alerted her that some large animal was approaching. Quickly rolling over and sitting up, she felt the hot rush of blood redden her face for the second time this morning. There stood Albert, not ten feet away, silent, with a fearful, quiet look on his face. Lydia was briefly petrified, but soon gained her feet and her composure. "Albert McGee! How dare you sneak up on me! If I had my father's pistol, I'd have shot you dead!"

"You would have too, wouldn't you?" The hint of a smile curved the edge of Albert's mouth, somehow making him look more frightening than before. Albert laughed and walked toward her.

"You take one step closer to me at your own risk, Albert McGee. My father will have you horsewhipped." Albert held his hands up in the air, like she already had the gun pointed at his heart.

"Simmer down, Lydia." He made a mock bow to humiliate her further. "What a little spitfire you are. No need to worry. I wouldn't touch you if you were the last unmarried girl in Kentucky."

"Well, that suits me perfectly, Albert McGee."

Lydia stood with her back straight, shoulders squared, menace in every inch of her five-foot frame. "Now, you best get on back home. I have too much to do to stand around jawboning with you all day."

Albert watched her standing there, smudges of dirt from her morning work on her face and clothes, her breath raising the swell of her breasts up and down with each cycle, fists clenched, one braid escaped from its rag tie allowing a bit of her bright mane of hair to untwist and catch in the breeze, green eyes ablaze with flecks of amber fire. No European queen clothed in gold and dripping with gems could ever have been half so beautiful or so terrifying. He clamped down tightly on the exasperation he always felt when he was around her and said softly, "Do you hate me so much, Lydia?"

For a second a hint of tenderness passed over Lydia's face. She unclenched her small fists and released some of the tension from her back and shoulders. Then, quick as that moment of sympathy came, it was gone. Lydia framed her words carefully, knowing they would be hurtful but wanting to dissuade Albert of his assumptions about her.

"I don't hate you, Albert. I am completely indifferent to you. Now go!" She pointed her finger toward the road, face flushed with emotion.

Albert's lip turned up again, and he gave her one last hungry look before he turned and ambled up the rise, feet and heart light, whistling a tune Lydia had never heard.

She watched him as he disappeared and then gave in to her conflicting feelings. Slumping down on the ground, she felt drained and tearful and baffled by the temporary madness that seemed to come over her around boys. Then, bending over the stream, she washed the salt trails off her face, wiped her hands on her apron, and headed back to the field. It was only then she gave thought to what Albert might have had in mind when he headed out to the spring. The logistics of his path had to have taken him right past Mama on her way back to the house. Her mind raced frantically over every imagined and unimaginable scenario as her hoe moved furiously over the garden plot. The sun was sinking low in the sky, and her stomach grumbled with neglect when she finished and headed back down the path to the house.

Pa was sitting on the front porch stoop when she arrived, working on knocking the day's mud off his boots. Jacob Ross acknowledged his daughter's approach with a slight lift of one eyebrow. They spoke in code these days. Lydia yearned for the easy conversations they used to have when she was a child. She took off her mud-caked shoes and washed her hands and face using water from the bucket on the front porch, then plopped down with her legs hanging from the old slatted swing, skirt hiked up almost to her knees.

"Lydia!" Her father's voice was sharp. "You are fifteen, not five. Do not sit like that! Cover yourself." Lydia knew better than to speak back to her father. She quickly stood up and let the skirt fall, but after the confused feelings of the day, once again a hot rush rose up from chest and rested like a cloud on her face. Her father didn't seem to notice her emotions as she pushed through the front door and up the stairs.

Her mother's voice caught her as she slammed the door to her room. "You better be back down those stairs in five minutes and help me get this meal ready for the men!" Lydia flopped on the bed with a force that would have broken it had her weight been as heavy as the burden she carried today. She felt a prisoner in her once familiar body, a stranger to her father, not to mention the eternally confusing troubled relationship with the mother who held her at arm's length.

After a few minutes she lifted herself wearily from the feather bed and walked to the window that faced her Uncle Jesse's house. She looked with longing at the well-worn path leading along the creek and disappearing into the stand of persimmon trees. Beyond that was a newly cultivated field her father and brothers had worked today and past that the creek twisted back, dividing her father's pasture from her Great-uncle Jesse's land. Her feet knew every step, her eyes every outcropping of limestone rock along the way. She breathed in and imagined the smell of the polish, leather, and musty paper in his parlor. Just one more sleep and the agony of a long-winded sermon tomorrow, and then she would be allowed an afternoon of escape curled in a cozy chair drinking in the knowledge from Jesse's wonderful books.

The remains of the day painted golden on the horizon reminded Lydia of her Uncle Jesse's promises. "Finish school with honors, Lydia, and I'll see to it you go to a real college. You're smarter than either of your brothers and you have the thirst in you. You weren't meant to be just a farmer's wife, and it's a new world for women who have the courage and strength to try." That new world was exactly what Lydia yearned for, somewhere beyond the narrowness and constant toil of farm life, a place where she could start to change the world for the better.

JESSE'S WORDS lay on her heart all through the school year, and she worked as she never had before despite the confusing annoyance of Albert's attention and her growing attraction to the more astute Duncan. It was clear Duncan felt the same about her, but finding a minute without Albert breathing down his neck had become impossible. Then came the day at lunch when Lydia had a brilliant idea. If trying to discourage him did not work, why not try the opposite? First she pulled her friend Beth aside and motioned for Duncan to join them quickly while Albert was still having a conversation with Rachel, who was trying to persuade him to share the ginger cake she had packed in her lunch.

"I have a plan, but I'm going to need help from you both," Lydia whispered.

As they listened to the plot, they observed Albert's feigned disdain for Rachel's blatant flirtation.

"I think it might just work," Beth said, "but what about Jacob and Josiah?"

"I was hoping you could talk to your sister about releasing the younger students a half hour early each day so those of us who are older get a bit longer instruction time."

"You are a genius," Duncan exclaimed. "She will be all for it!"

The next Monday morning it had all been arranged. Lydia packed an extra ham biscuit and tucked some of her mother's famous plum tarts into her lunch basket. Then she shocked Albert by asking if he wanted to eat lunch with her. Rachel always tried to coerce Albert into sharing her lunch basket, and he usually did after looking longingly at Lydia. As a stunned Albert was walking away with Lydia, Beth grabbed Rachel's hand and asked if she wanted to come eat with her. Then Beth smiled sweetly and pointed to a spot under a nearby tree where Duncan and Beth's boyfriend, James, were already settled. Rachel looked at them and then at Albert and Lydia walking away laughing. She had a moment of unrest before she tossed her curls and headed to secure a seat by Duncan. That afternoon, as Beth and Lydia walked slowly home together, Duncan caught up with them before the turn off to Beth's farm. Beth smiled and gave Lydia a hug; then she headed off toward home while Lydia walked on with Duncan for two miles to her house.

Rachel was flattered that the boy who had previously disregarded her was now openly sweet on her. Albert strutted around like the cock of the yard bragging that Lydia had finally given in to his charms. There was only one little thing. Albert and Rachel both lived to the east of school and had to take the same path home each day. Albert couldn't help but notice that the previously amorous Rachel was totally ignoring him. He found himself taking the occasional side glance at her black curls and frequently noticing her well-developed figure. "How odd," he thought to himself. "She never asks me to sit with her at lunch anymore." Shrugging, he gave it no further thought as he much preferred the formerly indifferent Lydia. He strutted around the school yard like the cock of the walk and congratulated himself for finally winning her over.

One morning Beth and Lydia were talking before school started. Duncan slipped up behind them and put his hand on Lydia's shoulder.

"How did you know this scheme with Rachel and Albert would work so well, Lydia?" Beth and Duncan both looked expectantly at her.

"It was clear they are both motivated by competition. The more I pushed Albert away, the more he tried to get my attention. Because he discounted her, Rachel became so determined to win him, she threw herself in his path. They both wanted the thing that was hard to get. I also knew that Rachel would jump at the chance to try to make Albert jealous by sitting with you, Duncan."

The three friends giggled quietly. It was working perfectly. Lydia had even noted that Albert often gazed longingly over at Rachel when she was hanging onto Duncan at lunch, giving Rachel the idea that she was successful in making Albert jealous. In her overconfidence it never occurred to her that the scheme was not of her own manufacture. Albert, too, seemed completely oblivious to the small deception.

As for Lydia and Duncan, the stolen half hour each day was the true beginning of their courtship. At first they mostly talked about their pasts, the loss of people they loved, but soon all their dreams and hopes spilled out. Before long they began to talk about the shared tomorrow they would have after graduation. They would move to Chicago where both could go to college. Duncan wanted to start his own business, and Lydia still longed to see the world and write about all the things she saw. They would combine their desires by starting an international company, maybe importing exotic merchandise from around the world.

Their steps often slowed on the way home, especially as they grew closer to Lydia's house. When her mother complained about her tardiness, she claimed it was due to long conversations with Beth, who she knew would cover for her. As the months passed, she came to an understanding with Duncan. They were two minds with one soul, one heart. Sometimes she caught her mother looking at her obvious happiness and cooperation with suspicion, and she had to suppress a smile.

Not being able to see Duncan on Saturday made it her least favorite day of the week. Sunday was better because at least Duncan was at church, even though she had to hide her interest in him from her parents. She always enjoyed the first fifteen minutes of church. She was able to sit idle with no one expecting her to jump up and fetch or clean something. The second fifteen minutes she began to grow restless and fidgety. As the last long hours slid slowly by, she almost yearned for a chore in order to get up off the hard bench. She tried to catch Duncan's eye several times, but with Albert sitting right beside him, she did not want the wrong boy to think she was interested.

When the final prayer was over and everyone started talking, she was able to slip close enough to Duncan to touch his hand briefly and then walk out the back. She ducked around the corner of the church and waited. Lydia smiled happily when he joined her a few minutes later, but her smile disappeared when she saw the expression on his face. "What is it, Duncan? You look like your best friend just died."

"Might as well have, Lydia," Duncan spoke in a most somber voice. "We're leaving. My sister had an offer of marriage from a friend she knew back east. He's from our hometown in Massachusetts, but he lives in Chicago now. They have been writing back and forth for some time, and she says he's a great catch."

Lydia's face dropped. "But you don't have to go with her, Duncan. Can't you stay here?" Even as she said it, she realized the absurdity of a fourteen-year-old living on his own in rural Kentucky when he could go to Chicago and attend the finest schools.

"You know the answer, Lydia. I've been over this in my head a thousand different ways trying to figure out another outcome. Nothing else makes sense than to go with my sister. She's my only family, and I know and like her fiancée. He'll make sure I can finish school. I know it's best, but, Lydia, I can't stand the thought of leaving you." Duncan blushed at declaring his feelings. "But we can write letters, and when we're of age we can . . ."

Just then Albert, who had been eavesdropping from around the corner, spoke up.

"You can what, Duncan? Trying to steal my girl, are you? Not going to happen, especially with you off in Chicago." Albert smirked. "No need to worry. I'll take good care of Lydia."

"Albert McGee. I've had it with you spying on me! Come on, Duncan, walk with me." She left a surprised Albert standing there while Duncan followed her to the front of the church, within sight of her parents but not in earshot. "Can you meet me on the lane to my Uncle Jesse's house this afternoon?" It was the only place she could think of that would not arouse suspicion in her parents and that Albert would not know about.

Duncan smiled shyly. "I'll be there as soon as I can get away after dinner." When Lydia looked up, she saw her mother moving in her direction with a disapproving stare. Lydia hurried toward the shade tree where the team was hitched and pulled herself up into the bed of the wagon. Seeing Ma leaving, Pa and the boys soon followed. Ma's mouth was a thin line that seemed to be struggling to find some critical words to speak, but in the end she quietly stored up her thoughts in anticipation of using them as ammunition in the future. Pa and the boys might as well have been on the moon for all they knew about the silent battle unfolding right in front of them.

The dinner dishes were washed, table clean, and the kitchen tidy when Lydia lifted her bonnet off the hook and onto her head. "I'm off to Jesse's." She threw the words over her shoulder as she headed out the door.

"Take Josiah with you, Lydia." Ma's second sense seemed to kick in when Lydia needed some privacy, but she knew better than to complain.

"Great idea!" Lydia said. Josiah perked up immediately, excited to be allowed to go on an adventure with his sister. Lydia would have to figure out how to keep the meeting with Duncan private later.

As it turned out, it was actually pretty simple. Josiah was racing ahead waving a stick saber he had picked up when she spotted Duncan standing in the lane. Duncan slipped behind a big oak before Josiah spotted him. "Race you to Uncle Jesse's porch, Josiah!" Lydia yelled as she started running. Josiah took off like a shot, laughing as he ran. Lydia slowed as soon as she reached the oak tree.

Duncan shyly reached for her hand, but once they touched, both were surprised to find themselves in an embrace and then a sweet first kiss. Flushed, they backed away awkwardly. Duncan spoke boldly. "I know it's a lot to ask of you, Lydia, but please wait for me. I love you with all my heart. Being with you has been like a wonderful dream. I would marry you now if I could. It's going to take a few years, but we'll write to each other, and I promise I'll come back for you as soon as I am of age. Will you, Lydia?"

"With all my heart, Duncan. I love you too. You are everything I want in my life. If only we had one more year, we could be married here. I promise I'll wait. Just write to me and let me know when you're coming."

Duncan pulled her back into his arms for another kiss. This one less awkward and less sweet, pulling her tight against him as she pressed into his body passionately. The promise of it left them both breathless and wanting more. As he reluctantly pulled away, she thought, yes, this was the stranger her mother tried to warn her against and now she understood why. The danger was not Duncan but her own desire for him.

Neither wanted to be the first to turn away. Finally Lydia said, "I'll count to three and then we both run as fast as we can."

Duncan nodded and Lydia started counting. "One, two, three . . ."

Neither of them moved. Then Lydia heard Josiah shouting in the distance. Duncan took a few steps backward and Lydia did the same. Then they both turned at the same time and started running, Duncan toward home, Lydia toward Uncle Jesse's. Tears were falling down Lydia's cheeks when she reached the familiar house. It would be four long years before Duncan would be eighteen.

The road ahead seemed long and frightening. How would she bear it?

SIX

JESSE'S LAST ADVENTURE

"I THINK DYING young might be best. Living so long and watching friends drop off one by one . . ." Jesse trailed off here, sank down further into the feather bed, and shut his eyes. "There will be no one to mourn me, Lydia."

"You know that's not true, Uncle Jesse," Lydia replied, sobbing. "I love you so. Don't leave me yet. You've always been my hero, the only one who truly believes in me."

Jesse reached a shaky wrinkled hand out to pat Lydia's arm. "Then you have to believe in yourself, my dear. Every gambler knows that confidence is what wins the game."

Lydia leaned over and put her head on Jesse's quilt. The events of the past few weeks flickered through her brain. The trip to Louisville with Jesse was a dream come true after years of promises. She still wondered what Pa had said or done to get Ma to relent and let her go. She doubted if it had anything to do with her graduating from school with the highest awards in the class, as Ma was never impressed. She just shook her head and asked how Lydia thought her gold stars were going to help her keep house or raise youngsters. She had helped Lydia with some of the finer points of making a new dress to wear for graduation, however. Ma encouraged any domestic skill. In fact, the closest Lydia had ever come to getting a compliment from Ma was for her neat and tidy stitching. The making of the dress had nevertheless been a tug of war between them as always.

It did not help that it had been Jesse who gifted her with the bolt of cloth for Christmas, cornflower blue with a tiny white flower print. The always impatient Lydia had started working on it right away using the pattern she found in the tattered copy of *Goody's Ladies Book* she discovered in Jesse's library. The book was several years old, but it was the closest thing to style she had ever seen. Her normal shapeless garments with cover-up pinafores were childish and unflattering. This was a real woman's dress, the kind she saw the ladies who passed through town on the stagecoach wear.

Once the style of the dress began to take shape, Ma accused Lydia of "going above her raising" and trying to "put on airs." Lydia bit her tongue and kept working, fashioning the waist to fit close to her body and flatter her bustline. The separate skirt contained the bulk of the fabric and its wide flare, along with multiple petticoats, was clearly impractical for life on a dirt farm in Kentucky. To Lydia that was the best part of the dress. It was meant for wearing in the world where she wanted to live, far from this tiny backwater and these people with their small ideas.

She began to rethink her big plans when they arrived in Louisville, however. It was much more terrifying than she had imagined, but not a soul would have guessed by her demeanor. Having Uncle Jesse by her side allowed her to put on a show of confidence. She realized, without him she would have just stood and gaped like the little country girl she was. She wrote everything about the trip down in her journals, starting with packing her valise, the coach ride to Elizabethtown, and the train ride on the new L&N to Louisville. She clung close to Uncle Jesse on the train and prayed that if she died on this journey, it would be on the return trip.

More than once during the trip, grown men gave Lydia looks that made her uncomfortable. Uncle Jesse did not feel the need to explain to anyone why a well-dressed old man with a walking stick had a beautiful auburn-haired girl in the first blush of youth on his arm. The desk clerk at the Galt House Hotel made an obvious effort to be discreet when Uncle Jesse asked for two rooms, one for him and one for his niece. Lydia's attempt to look innocent and above reproach most likely made her look even more guilty. She was fighting back tears by the time they reached their adjoining rooms. Jesse seemed oblivious to her distress. He just tipped the bellhop and told Lydia he needed to rest and clean up before dinner and suggested she do the same.

Never having had a room of her own, Lydia quickly recovered her composure and twirled about looking in every drawer (empty), checking out the view (the Ohio River) and the bed (soft and luxurious). She unpacked her valise, filled up the drawers, and hung her only other dress in the wardrobe. Feeling dusty from the road, she took off her good dress, shook it, and checked for any spots. Then she poured water from the pitcher into her bowl and cleaned herself using the soft hotel linen and the bar of Pears soap they supplied. Feeling refreshed, Lydia dressed again and stretched across the bed with her journal to fill in the events of the day.

She had no idea she had been sleepy until the knock at the door awakened her. Half-asleep she hurried to open it. To her surprise it was not Uncle Jess standing there but the man who had brought her bags up earlier, now with a note for her in his hand. She opened it and read, "Meet me downstairs in the dining room for dinner." Lydia shooed the bellhop away without a tip as she had no money and was ignorant of customs. She adjusted the pins in her hair, pinched her cheeks in the mirror, and then, feeling acceptable, she headed downstairs.

She was surprised to find that Uncle Jesse was not alone in the restaurant. They were joined for dinner by a man a little younger than her uncle who rose and introduced himself as Stuart Simon from Southern Kentucky College, which had opened recently in Hopkinsville. The evening was spent quite pleasantly with a wonderful meal of chicken fricassee with mashed potatoes and cabbage plus apple dumplings for dessert. The best part of the evening was the conversation full of history and literature and politics with her opinions being solicited and entertained.

As the dining room emptied, Lydia suddenly realized how tired Uncle Jesse looked. "Oh dear, I think it's getting very late. If you gentlemen will excuse me, I must head to my room." Both of them immediately stood and apologized for keeping her up, but she noted a look of relief on her uncle's face.

"Tomorrow we will take a tour of the city, my dear, so we do need our rest. Thank you so much for joining us, Mr. Simon," Uncle Jesse said as the men shook hands.

"The pleasure was all mine, Mr. Ross. Lydia is a most unusual young lady with bright prospects." Mr. Simon gushed as he took Lydia's hand briefly. "Best of luck to you in your future."

On her way back to her room Lydia could think of nothing else but the future. The rumors of war they discussed seemed very distant. Not at all sleepy, she pulled out her journal eager to get down the conversation and the sights she had seen before she forgot any details. She lost track of time as she wrote until finally the coal oil lamp flickered and she realized she had burned through an extravagance of fuel. As always she wrote a page intended for Duncan, for although she had not heard from him since he left for Chicago, she never gave up hope that he was out there thinking of her as she thought of him. She slipped into her nightdress, crawled under the covers, and slept the sleep of the innocent with dreams of a million possible futures flitting through her head. In every dream Duncan was there, arms open and waiting for her to explain why he could not get to her sooner.

The next day Uncle Jesse took her on a marvelous tour of Louisville, Broadway Street, the majestic courthouse, the racetrack, and the school for the blind. The one place she would never forget was the slave market along the waterfront. There was a small light-skinned girl of about ten years standing naked except for a sort of loincloth around her waist. A rough jute rope encircled her neck that was rubbed raw, with the other end in the hand of the auctioneer. An expression of powerlessness was etched on her face. It was as if she was absent from her body and watching the scene from afar.

Lydia tried to turn her face away, but Uncle Jesse took note and told her she needed to watch, to be a witness to history. "Do not look away and pretend that this baby is less than human, Lydia. Always remember what you saw here today," Uncle Jesse said gently. "Most of these very light-skinned children were sired by a plantation owner. It's usually the owners' wives who demand the children are sold to remove the daily evidence of their husbands' indiscretions."

Lydia swallowed down the bile that rose in her throat and kept her eyes open.

"I promise, Uncle Jesse, I will never forget."

The next morning they boarded the train for the trip home. When they sat down in the compartment, Lydia noticed that Jesse's hand was shaky as he reached for hers. When she looked into his face, she saw that his skin was sallow, his eyes dull, and the wrinkles seemed to be etched deeper into his face. Alarmed, she said, "Jesse, you're not well. Shall I see if there is a doctor on the train?"

"No, no, dear, I'm just tired from the trip. We need to talk now. I want to tell you what Mr. Simon said. He is a teacher at Daughters College in Harrodsburg. He wants you to come there as a student in the fall. If that suits you, I will pay for your tuition and give you money to live on."

Jesse paused for Lydia's response. She almost shrieked with joy. "Oh, Uncle Jesse, nothing would make me happier. I will study hard and make you proud. I promise."

Uncle Jesse patted her soft young hand with his gnarled and spotted one. "Of that I am sure, my child. We will make it happen."

Now here she sat holding the same precious hand as his life slowly ebbed away. She felt a horrible guilt for the trip because Uncle Jesse had just seemed to keep going downhill after they returned. Weak as he was, he still wanted to talk. "I wrote a letter for you, Lydia. You will get it when I am gone. I put all my wishes in it. Everything will be as we planned."

"Oh, Jesse," Lydia sobbed, "the only thing I need is for you to get better."

"That is not in the cards, my dear. I am at peace with death. It's my last big adventure." He paused for a coughing fit, and just when Lydia thought he would not breathe again, she heard a deep raspy gasp. After a few minutes he continued weakly. "I have dreamed about my dear wife and my mother and father every night for the last few weeks. Sometimes even when I think I am awake they come to me, holding out their hands, begging me to join them."

Lydia did not reply, and they sat in silence for long minutes. "Jesse," she said softly, "do you believe that we live again? I know it sounds like heresy, but some of the wisest men who ever lived believed it, like Plato. Remember when we read his books?" Jesse did not reply, so Lydia went on. "I hope we do, Uncle Jesse, because I want to find you again on this earth, not sitting on some cloud playing on a harp."

She was startled for a minute but finally realized that the sound she heard coming from Uncle Jesse was a laugh, a ragged belly laugh ending in another fit of coughing. When he was able to speak again, he had a weak smile on his face. "Oh my darling girl. You are always full of surprises. God likely does not need another harpist, and if he does there are people more qualified. Let me tell you this, when my family who have gone on come to me, they seem happy and busy. I know your great-grandmother Lydia is surely not going to spend eternity doing nothing. If I have learned anything in this life, it's that God has many faces. I am looking forward to meeting whatever manifestation is forthcoming."

Lydia took a long look at the man she had loved all her life, the one who had always been there for her. He was tired, bone tired of living and waiting. She could not be so selfish as to hold him here when he had places to go. She gave him a kiss on the cheek. "You best be standing looking for me when I come, Uncle Jesse. You will need to introduce me to all the people you have told me about all these years."

"I promise, my darling girl. I'll be there." Jesse closed his eyes. "I need to rest now, sweetheart. Send your father in and let me talk to him a minute. Then I need to sleep."

Lydia came out of the bedroom and saw them all standing like crows on a fencerow waiting to eat the corn that was being sown. She knew her papa loved Jesse and so did Uncle Will, but her mother had no use for him. Her brothers, Jacob and Josiah, were not especially close to Jesse, although Josiah honored him because Lydia did. The busy country doctor had already done all he could and was antsy to get on to other things. Papa and the doctor rose and went into the bedroom. They came back after a short time and the doctor simply said, "He's gone."

FOR THE NEXT few days Lydia barely had time to cry. There were arrangements to be made, neighbors to be notified. They had to wait for the Methodist circuit rider to come and hold the service. Albert came to the funeral dressed in a new dark suit with an ascot at his neck. He took Lydia's arm and walked with her through the church and to the hill where Jesse was laid to rest beside his beloved wife.

Dazed with the loss, Lydia accepted Albert's comforting arm. Not having heard a word from Duncan in the two long years since he had moved to Chicago, she found herself turning more to Albert. He fit himself contentedly into the family, courting them as much as her. It made no difference anyway because Jesse had promised her that she would be going to college, that he would make a way. She waited for the will and the promised letter.

She was still waiting almost a month later when all of Jesse's household goods had been sorted and her Uncle Will had taken over Jesse's farm. Lydia knew Will and his family would be moving there soon. Everything seemed to be apace except it was getting closer to the day when school would start in Harrodsburg and nothing had been arranged. Determined, Lydia confronted her parents at supper. "I need to see the letter Uncle Jesse left me about school."

Her mother answered too quickly with an almost practiced surprise, "I have no idea what you're talking about. Jesse didn't leave any letter for you." Lydia turned to her father for confirmation, but he did not raise his eyes, just kept looking at the venison stew he was eating.

"Papa, Uncle Jesse told me on his deathbed that he left me a letter explaining everything. I'm supposed to start school in Hopkinsville at the end of September. He promised."

"That fool old man!" her mother said. "Always making big promises he couldn't keep. There is no money for you to go off to school, Lydia. He probably spent the last of it on that ridiculous trip to Louisville. We had to sell off his goods to pay bills."

Lydia had heard the phrase *my heart dropped*, but she had never known what it meant until now. She studied the faces of her parents and her brothers sitting around the table looking for the lie. Josiah was guileless, Jake smirking, Ma triumphant. Her Pa would not meet her eyes directly. Lydia stood up from the table, picked up her shawl, and walked out the door. She heard noises from her mother, but the words blurred, something about dishes perhaps. She heard Pa say, "Let her go, Matilda."

It was dark when Josiah came to fetch her from Uncle Jesse's porch. She sat with her head on her knees, Belle leaning protectively against her. Josiah sat down quietly beside her and put his arm around her shoulders. Lydia had thought she was all cried out, but she leaned her head into her brother's chest and sobbed a bit more. He waited patiently, but finally he spoke, "Come on, Lydia. We have to go home. You can't sit here all night."

Slowly and silently, Lydia began to rise. Belle scrambled up beside her, happily whacking her enormous tail against her legs. She patted his head, and the beast looped off toward a home that had lost all meaning to Lydia in the last few hours, but there was no place else to go.

The next morning Lydia packed all of her journals in her valise and shoved it far back under her bed.

SEVEN
SETTLING FOR LESS

Gradually Lydia came to terms with the loss of Jesse, but she could not justify the lies he told. Perhaps her mother was right, and he was just a tired old man with impossible dreams. Her imaginings took her to dark brooding places where she questioned the compass she had followed steadfastly for so long. Thinking her self-esteem could not sink further, she decided to try to reach Duncan one last time. When he first left, she had faithfully composed letters to him each week and handed them to her father to post. Months went by without a word in reply. After a year Lydia just wrote her thoughts in her journals and kept her sorrow to herself. Maybe their feelings for each other had been her own fantasy, too, but she needed to find out now more than ever.

She worked on the letter for days, pouring out her heart and asking for his advice and comfort. She brought the letter down to breakfast one Saturday morning and asked Pa to mail it when he went into town. He looked at the letter, then at Lydia, and stuffed it down into his overall pocket without a word.

It was about two months later that Pa tossed a folded letter down on the supper table.

"Lydia, this came for you a while back. I know you have been upset and I didn't want you to feel any worse, so I opened it. I'm afraid it's bad news, but you need to know."

Lydia braced herself and picked up the letter. There was no envelope and the writing was not familiar. It was very brief.

My dear Lydia,

    You don't know me but I am Duncan's brother-in-law. Sorry to be the bearer of bad news, but I need to tell you that we lost Duncan to typhoid last winter. It would be best not to get in touch with my wife as she is very fragile these days.

    Yours sincerely,

    Maxwell Carpenter

For long minutes Lydia tried to take in the news. She pictured Duncan standing beside her at the church, twisting his hat in his hands, telling her he was leaving. Then she thought of the secret meeting they had that afternoon right before he headed off for Chicago. With Albert finally nowhere around, Duncan had declared his feelings for her. Taking her in his arms, he had kissed her, her very first kiss. It was sweet and gentle and full of meaning. The next one was passionate and real and full of promise. How could all that love be gone from the earth forever? Uncle Jesse was old and ready to leave, but Duncan was young and full of hope and dreams for the future, dreams he wanted to share with her.

Matilda took it as a good sign that Lydia did not cry. She overlooked the obvious as usual; her daughter had simply reached a grief overload, and all she felt in this moment was numbness.

Albert had been showing up for Sunday dinner with some regularity, but in the past few months while Lydia waited for her reply, he became a fixture around the table. Lydia had little to say to him, but her Ma and Pa treated him like their son-in-law. Night after night Lydia dreamed about a river. She always stood on the bank looking down into the muddy waters fighting the urge to jump. Then she would look up, and across the distance of the broad channel she could clearly see Uncle Jesse and Duncan beckoning to her. Just as she would start to jump, she would wake with a start.

She sometimes thought about her journals tucked under the bed, but she no longer had the heart to write about things that would never come true. She was civil to Albert at first, but gradually she began to try to take an interest in the things he was saying, and he seemed to be listening intently to her too. One Sunday afternoon he asked her to take a ride with him in his buggy. She glanced toward her ma and pa, and they both nodded their approval. Albert helped her into the wagon and started off in the direction of his parents' farm.

Curious, Lydia asked him, "Are we visiting with your family today, Albert?"

"No, I have a surprise for you." Albert smiled but was clearly not going to be forthcoming about where they were headed. Lydia did not probe.

The dappled grey trotted patiently up the rutted road to the McGee farm and objected briefly when Albert turned the buggy down a fresh path. It was wooded and cool under the trees that lined the narrow trail up the hill. At the top the woods opened up, and Albert pointed to a spot in the valley. There, nestled up against a wooded area facing a broad open field was a clearing. In that clearing someone had started building a structure.

"What is it, Albert?" Lydia was puzzled. If it was to be a barn, it was too far from his parents' house to be watched over.

Albert started in on a brief but well-rehearsed speech. "You have to know you are the only girl I have ever been serious about. If you will have me, I want this to be our home. I need you, Lydia. Will you marry me?"

"I . . . I . . . ," stammered Lydia. "I don't know what to say,

Albert. I guess I shouldn't be surprised, but I am. Can you give me some time to think about it?"

Albert's face darkened for a brief second, but he held back his annoyance. "Of course, sweetheart. Let's go look at the layout of the house. It might help you say yes."

A few hours later Albert dropped Lydia off at her parents' house. Everyone jumped up when she came in the door. They all looked at her in anticipation. Lydia realized she had been the last to know about Albert's intentions today.

"Well?" Her mom leaned in eagerly. "Do you have any news?"

Lydia attempted to conceal her irritation but saw no point in being coy. "I did not give him an answer. I need to think about it."

"Whatever is there to think about? He is a hard-working Christian man. He has a farm and livestock, and he is building you a house."

She looked at them all waiting for her to speak. Everything in her brain wanted to scream in frustration. Ma was right. She had no other options except to remain a spinster living with her parents. Perhaps a life with Albert wouldn't be so bad, but things kept coming at her so fast. "I need to sleep on it," Lydia said. "I'll give him an answer soon."

That night she dreamed again of the river. This time the far bank seemed miles and miles away with hundreds of people gathered on the other shore. She could not make out Jesse or Duncan on the other side. She heard a noise behind her and turned. There stood Albert and all her family waiting for her, except all of them had eyes like wild beasts and their hands ended in claws instead of fingers. Lydia woke shaking with an inaudible scream caught in her throat.

The next Sunday when Albert came to dinner, he asked her for her answer at the table. Lydia looked around at all their eager eyes and shuttered thinking of the nightmare. Then shrugging her shoulders and lowering her head, she whispered a tiny "yes." Ma, Pa, and

Albert cheered, and they set the wedding date for June when the house would be ready. Later when she lay in her bed, she was glad that no one spoke of love. She did not want to begin her marriage with a lie.

IN THE WEEKS ahead Ma was happier than Lydia had ever seen her. She ordered yard goods for new clothes and linens, and both of them sewed all through the late winter and early spring months. When Lydia questioned her on where the money for all this was coming from, she said she and Pa had set aside a bit for her wedding long ago. Lydia drew the line at a white wedding dress like the one Queen Victoria wore. She picked a practical pale-green organza with a drop shoulder and three-quarter flared sleeve. The waist looked impossibly small, but Ma had to take it in a week before the wedding because Lydia had shed so much weight off of an already tiny figure. Ma scolded her for not eating more and tried to tempt her with treats, but Lydia had no appetite.

The morning of her wedding Lydia woke to the familiar sound of the rooster. In that brief moment between sleep and waking she lived in a world where Jesse was still alive, she was happily in college, and Duncan was waiting for her to finish so they could marry. The shock of the day came on her soon enough. They were all to gather in the church at ten for the ceremony, and after they would have a meal with the family in Lydia and Albert's new house. She had not been there since it was finished, and all the family insisted they would have everything set up for her and fix the meal so she did not have to raise a finger.

Albert's smile when he saw her was reassuring, but she found herself frozen in place at the back of the church. Pa finally tugged at her arm and said, "Come on, Lydia, time to get married." Everything in her heart told her no. Did all brides feel this way? Wasn't she supposed to be joyful? All she saw in front of her were happy smiling faces. She finally took her first stumbling step down the aisle to the place where destiny had steered her.

L<small>YDIA HAD NOT REALLY THOUGHT MUCH</small> about what to expect from her wedding night. She had no one to ask except her mother, who just told her she would get used to it. She and Beth had guessed a bit about the logistics, but they did not know one older married girl who could actually enlighten them. They all spoke in generalities and the information they provided was inconsistent. Beth's older cousin blushed and giggled but made it clear that she enjoyed time spent alone with her husband. Lydia decided she would stop over-thinking it and trust that her new husband would be patient.

So far Albert had carefully avoided pushing her for any physical contact in the scattered moments when they had been alone in the months since their engagement. He would give her a chaste broth-erly peck on the cheek when he dropped her at home, but that was the extent of his affections. She never initiated anything with him or even questioned his lack of interest, but she did recall the few kisses she had greedily shared with Duncan years ago. Her hope was that Albert was being more cautious, more disciplined, and holding back until they were married. When the minister told him he could kiss the bride, it was the first time his lips had actually come in direct contact with hers. Nothing anyone had said or she had imagined prepared her for the pain and humiliation Albert visited upon her that night.

It started right after the wedding breakfast was over and the few family and friends had taken their leave. She stood in the doorway waving good-bye to the retreating buggies and wagons. When she turned back into the house, Albert closed the front door, grabbed her arm, and pulled her roughly into the bedroom. She laughed nervously and tried to tease Albert asking if she could at least put on her new nightgown. Instead, he turned her around and pushed her down on the bed, lifted the skirt of her new gown, explored between her legs with rough fingers, and then pushed himself into her urgently.

When she started crying, he drove himself into her more forcefully and whispered in her ear, "You're mine to do with as I wish now. A few tears aren't going to stop me." In a few minutes he collapsed on top of her with the full weight of his body. Unable to get her breath, she started struggling, and he lifted himself up for a moment and made an attempt to start thrusting again. Fortunately he was spent for the moment, so he stood up and let her slide off the bed sobbing. He methodically took off his new suit, hung it neatly over the bedroom chair, and then pulled her up from the floor.

"Undress for me," he demanded. Lydia started shaking her head no. His look was dark and frightening when he said, "You want me to tear it off for you?"

Sobbing, Lydia started removing her beautiful new dress bit by bit as he sat on the bed and watched. She tried not to look him in the eye as she did it. When she was finally naked, he stood and started roughly handling and pinching her breasts, her bottom, and pushing his finger crudely between her legs. He withdrew his hand and smiled to find it tinted with blood. Finally, having tortured her for as long as he wanted and satisfied that he was the first man to have her, he pushed her on the bed to mount her again. "Now you know how I have felt for years now while you teased and played me. I watched you flirt with Duncan Porter and how all those other boys looked at you. You thought I was a fool, didn't you?"

Lydia was too terrified to speak a word of protest. When she was sure he was asleep, she got up quietly, washed, and put on the beautiful hand-tatted white nightgown she and her Ma had made for the wedding night. She walked through the unfamiliar house and touched all the familiar furniture that had been taken from Uncle Jesse's. At breakfast she had tried to ask her ma and pa about the pieces she thought were sold and gone, but their answers were vague. She finally settled into her familiar old friend, the green velvet wing chair where she had spent so many happy hours reading and talking to Jesse. Pulling the throw from the back of the chair over her, she sat staring into the nothing looming in front of her until she finally fell asleep. It was barely dawn when Albert pulled her up out of her safe place and back to the bedroom for a new round of "wifely duty," which was only slightly less painful than the first time.

When her ma and pa dropped in on her unexpectedly a few weeks later, Lydia was far from the picture of a happy blushing bride. She was in a not-too-clean smock dress, hair unbrushed, with dark circles under her eyes. The house was unkempt, dishes in the sink, floors covered in mud Albert had tracked around carelessly. Pa was frankly startled by her appearance and nudged Ma to talk to her while he went outside to find Albert. As soon as her Pa went out of the door, her mother started scolding her.

"For goodness' sake, Lydia, you are setting some kind of record for letting yourself go. I want you to get up this minute and go wash your face, brush and fix your hair, and put on a clean dress. I'll start in this kitchen until you come join me. I brought supper for us all that just needs to be warmed. Lord, there is not even a fire in the stove. This will not do!"

The look on Lydia's face when she turned to her mother was frightening. "Ma," she whispered, "why didn't you tell me how awful it would be lying with a man?"

"Oh for goodness' sake, Lydia, why do you always have to be so dramatic? For the life of me I can't understand why Albert has put up with you. Most men would beat a wife who kept such a poor house." Lydia looked down at the bruises on her wrists. She knew her mother had seen them too. She wondered why she had bothered to say anything to her mother, then rose in resignation to do as she was told.

She moved like a clockwork bird, jerkily willing her body into motion. She spoke in mumbles but came back in a short while looking more put together but with the same tortured sadness on her face. Ma had the fire going and the stew she brought sitting on the stove. Lydia went to the sink and started cleaning dishes while Ma swept up and tidied the room. Soon the table was set and ready with Ma's bubbling stew, fresh bread, and a circle of creamy butter.

Albert came in whistling. "You do set a great table, Ma Ross. I sure will be glad when Lydia learns to cook as good as you. Nothing but burnt biscuits and underdone meat this week." Albert let out a laugh. Ma and Pa looked awkwardly at Lydia knowing her to be an excellent cook.

Finally it was Ma who broke the silence. "Takes a while to learn a new kitchen, Albert. She'll be just fine in a week or two. Won't you, Lydia?"

She responded obediently, "Yes, Ma. I'm sorry, Albert. I just need to get used to the stove."

Ma stayed to help Lydia clean up while Pa and Albert sat in the parlor talking politics. Pa noticed that Albert had appropriated Uncle Jesse's chair.

As soon as they were out of sight of the house, Jacob spoke, "Mattie, what's wrong with Lydia? Did she say anything about the way Albert was treating her?"

"I spoke to her, Jacob. Her expectations for marriage were unrealistic. Too many romantic notions from all those books she read. She will snap out of it now, I'm sure." Matilda's tone was stern.

"I spoke to Albert," Jacob replied. "Asked him to be patient since Lydia has been through so much this past year. He seemed a little embarrassed, and I believe he will try harder. We'll check back with them before too long."

Matilda retorted heatedly, "I would not put any blame on Albert. Lydia has always been headstrong. She needs a firm hand. If we had not stepped in, she might have run off with that worthless Duncan Porter."

Jacob chose his words carefully. "I still don't think what we did was right, Matilda, lying to our own flesh and blood, when her heart was already broken over Jesse's death."

Matilda's voice became shriller as she spoke. "For heaven's sake, Jacob. Do not bring it up again. It was for her own good! The money Jesse left would have been wasted. Lydia would have ended up ruined. No God-fearing man would want her if she were to go to college. If she married Duncan Porter, she would have run off to some big city and you would never see her again. We need her here where we can keep an eye on her, Jacob!"

After long years married to Matilda, Jacob had learned when it was best to stop pushing a topic. He loved Matilda dearly, and despite her notions concerning their only daughter, he knew she truly believed what she was doing was best. Perhaps he should have put his foot down years ago, but the pattern was set now and it was too late to change. He drove the rest of the way home in guilty silence.

EIGHT

BABIES AND WAR

ALBERT AND LYDIA rarely had a conversation, so it was surprising that they eventually came to an accommodation. He had played out most of his anger in the first weeks, and Lydia was cowed. After the shock of all her loss, she seemed to have also relinquished the strong will that had kept her moving forward for so long. Having grown up in a house with little talking about emotions, the lack of communication didn't seem abnormal to Lydia, but she had hoped for so much more.

Her mother had emphasized that marriage required compromise and she needed to let go of her silly notions and make a home for her husband. After the visit by her ma and pa, she started making more of an effort and soon pulled herself out of the total despair she had felt right after the wedding. Albert became less demanding after her cooking improved, and she started taking better care of herself and the house. Lydia quickly learned that the best way to avoid pain during sex was to lie still and be quiet. Their contact gradually became a quick and impersonal interlude a few times a week.

By the time their first Christmas rolled around, Lydia had even put a few badly needed pounds back on. Her old nemesis, Rachel

Renfrow, had given her one of those insults masquerading as a compliment at church last week: "You sure look a lot better with a bit of weight on you, Lydia. We were all beginning to worry you had the consumption." She always found it strange that women felt the need to try to make themselves look better by making other women look worse. Rachel was not yet over Lydia "stealing" Albert from her as if there was some kind of competition. If it had been a contest, Lydia surely did not think she could possibly be the winner.

It was late March when Albert remarked on her weight. It was not uncomplimentary, just an aside comment as she was dressing one morning that she looked healthier. Albert was more likely to notice something about one of his mules than his wife, so Lydia took it to heart.

She could not think how she might be gaining since she had felt so sick a lot over the winter. Now that spring was in the air, she had begun to feel a bit better. Lydia was well into her morning chores when her ma and pa showed up at the door. Although the distance between the farms was short, they rarely stopped by for a visit. Lydia put the kettle on, pulled out cups, and started looking to see if Albert had left any of the shortcakes she had made last week. As she was looking, Pa had left and come back in with a large basket loaded with food.

Ma directed him to set it on the table. "Brought you some of that ham we cured and a few other things. How about some plum tarts right now?"

"Oh, I better not," Lydia said. "I'm hungry all the time these days, but Albert mentioned this morning that I'm putting on weight and I can't afford new clothes this time of year."

Matilda had watched her daughter eat like a hired hand and not gain an ounce, so she was immediately suspicious. After they had water on the boil and tarts set out on the table, Matilda suggested to Pa that he go check on Albert. As soon as he was gone, Ma looked at her sharply, "Have you been sick lately, Lydia?"

"Well, a bit this winter but much better now," she answered.

"When was the last time you had your monthly flow?" Ma queried further.

Lydia turned pale. "I don't recall. You know I sometimes miss it when I'm upset and life has been hectic for a long time now. You don't think I'm . . ."

"Expecting? Yes, Lydia, that's exactly what I think." Ma pummeled her with a dozen other symptoms, and Lydia had to answer yes to each one. Both of them went silent when Pa and Albert came in the front door.

Albert's voice echoed loudly in the quiet room. "Did I hear something about plum tarts?"

"Yes," Lydia answered grimly. "Have a seat and I'll get you some tea. I need to tell you something. And Ma, I think I might have one of those tarts now. "

BABY BOY JOSEPH AARON MCGEE was born on September 6, 1860. His easy birth seemed to disappoint her mother, but Ma and all of the family seemed overjoyed that he was male. When Lydia took the tiny bundle into her arms, all resentment about their attitudes faded. He was small, but sturdy, with a head of black hair and the tireless lungs of a politician. He was quiet only when she was nursing and rocking him in the chair Pa had made and given to her in advance of her coming birthday. In the wee hours as she held the baby, she read and reread the often outdated newspapers that were passed on to her from the nearest neighbor. The flicker of the coal oil lamp made it difficult to see the small print, but much of it was practically memorized after the many readings. She wondered about the old news concerning the upcoming presidential election, as it may have already been decided by the time the paper reached her.

While Lincoln was Kentucky born and a distant relative of the

McGees, he was not popular in his own land. He was considered a moderate, but his declaration that "this government cannot endure, permanently half slave and half free" made it clear to all that an ill wind was blowing across the country, one that most Kentuckians felt would surely harm them all. Not that many of her neighbors could afford to keep slaves, but all just seemed to want to keep things the way they were. In the end the politician John Bell carried Kentucky as expected, but when the national vote was counted, Lincoln was the victor. Joseph was cutting his first tooth by the time the account of the inauguration reached them. As Lydia nursed her baby boy, she kept thinking of the little girl she had seen in the auction block in Louisville. Because of the child's light skin, it was clear that the mother had been subject to the attentions of a man with absolute power over her. Even if the man was a brute, when the babe was born, did her heart not swell with love the same way Lydia's did for her son? Did the mother still grieve over the child who was lost to her forever?

Albert's family had no slaves, but the reasons were not from conviction nor concern for the welfare of black people. The land they owned was not suited for the cotton or tobacco cash crops of the Deep South. They grew some corn and hay to feed animals over the winter, but the cows they owned grew fat on the lush grasses that grew on their hilly land and the sheep munched happily on the hilly and rocky land unsuitable for cows or crops. The slave family that Lydia's great-grandmother freed long ago had sold the farm she had given them for a pittance to other family members and moved north to Illinois. Lydia adopted her Uncle Jesse's aversion to slavery based on his stories about her forward-thinking great-grandmother and the books she read that her mother deemed unsuitable for women.

Even though Lincoln got few votes in Kentucky, he was wise enough to know it was a key state to defend. Lydia read the news of the Union Army amassing in Bowling Green that spring. Rumors abounded concerning either Yankees or Rebels, depending on what neighbor you were talking to. Gossip about skirmishes and battles in Virginia and Tennessee caused anxiety and tension, but in the end the farm was neither strategically located nor rich enough for the storm of war to take heed of their small community.

When Lydia saw the news that first South Carolina then six other states had seceded from the Union, she was fearful of Kentucky joining them. As time passed, though, it seemed that while there was support for both sides of the conflict, most people in Kentucky leaned toward the Union. More importantly, despite the Union general's efforts to recruit the local men to enlist, only a few were willing to join into a battle led by outsiders.

Lydia yearned for conversation and communication from Albert. She often thought back to their school years when he had insisted on talking when she had no inclination. Now it seemed he had run out of words entirely. Even before marriage he had not been affectionate, but she had thought he was simply too respectful of her. Her wedding night had quickly proven her wrong about his regard for her virtue or intellect. She was too stunned after that to attempt to have a discussion about her feelings. After baby Joe was born, he had not troubled her for sex for six months. Then one night when she crawled in bed exhausted from getting the baby back to sleep, he was waiting for her. The act was performed quickly, silently, and mechanically. The assault on her body was perhaps more painful than their wedding night, and her tearful pleadings were ineffectual against the strength of his demand. Afterward she lay staring into the darkness, praying he would at least leave her alone for the rest of the evening. A few hours later she found the answer to her prayer was no.

On November 20, 1862, the day after her birthday and nine months to the day after Albert reclaimed her body, George Avery McGee arrived. Joseph had been a fussy colicky baby requiring her full time and attention. She had dreaded going through this again with little George, but he was a blessing. He slept through the night despite thunder or the shrill crying of his older brother, woke happy and cooing in the morning, and seemed delighted with any attention he was given.

Albert was pleased to have boys, but not much interested in them day to day until Joseph started walking and then talking. Joe was a precocious child both mentally and physically. By the time he was two, he and his brother were inseparable. Placid George would have been content to sit and play with a sunbeam, except he wanted to be where Joseph was, so he soon learned to crawl and then walk, often holding on to his brother's hand.

Lydia's beloved brother Josiah showed up one day in March of 1863 with a shy dark-haired young girl and introduced her as his soon-to-be wife, Mary. Lydia welcomed any distraction from the grim news about battles, skirmishes, and guerilla warfare. When Josiah and Mary married in a small ceremony a few weeks later in April, their brother Jake stood up as witness for him and caught the eye of Mary's rather forceful friend Suzanna. Jake had a reputation for being hotheaded which had put off all the ladies he had wooed previously, but after a brief and tempestuous courtship it was clear that Jake had met his match. Lydia was happy for her brothers as both seemed to have found someone well suited for them.

Mary's sweet, diplomatic nature was clear when she and Josiah moved in with Ma and Pa after they married. Lydia was relieved that Ma finally had the daughter she had wished for, the perfect wife, and within a year of their marriage a mother to a healthy little boy, born March of 1864. Jacob and Suzanna spent a brief time with Suzanna's parents, but with the war ending they were restless and wanted to find their own way. Suzanna's grandparents had a house and small general store in Bardstown. It had been the object of a few raids with some damage done. They were elderly, afraid of more trouble and unable to run the store or make repairs. Suzanna asked Jacob if he would be willing to move there to help. Jacob, who always had an eye out for his own advantage, made sure the elders wrote a will that left the place to the young couple when they passed away. Jacob had never been fond of farming, and he liked the idea of owning a business.

Before they left, Pa, Jacob, and Albert helped Josiah build his own house a few miles down the road from Ma and Pa. They still received news of battles, but they were happening far from western Kentucky. The men had avoided conscription, and despite the tumult of the divided states around them, life on the farm was something akin to normal. There were some shortages of items like sugar and dry goods, but at least no soldiers on either side came to raid their farms like the accounts they read in what papers still managed to find their way to the countryside.

It was very hard to be jealous of the ever sweet and undemanding Mary. Lydia was glad that her mother had someone else to focus on and the always compliant Mary did not seem to mind. Lydia would have welcomed a small bit of her mother's attention when she miscarried in the spring of 1864. It was hard hearing Ma tell her she needed to just get over it and be grateful for the healthy children she had. Mary, who was pregnant again, gave Lydia a look of pity when she heard Ma's harsh tone, but she held her tongue. Lydia had no expectations of sympathy from Albert, but she supposed he did the best he could by leaving her alone and letting her heal for a time.

August settled on them that summer with all its steamy, oppressive unpleasantness. The corn and wheat grew inches in a day, and the cattle sat up to their bellies in the watering pond. The horses walked slowly in circles around the big elm tree in the pasture following the shade as the sun moved across the sky. They all rose early trying to get chores done before the heat of the day. Some nights were barely cooler than midday with the air so still it was morning before the house cooled down enough to sleep.

Late one night Lydia grew tired of trying to find the cool side of the pillow. She slipped out of bed and into the yard where the smell of honeysuckle almost drowned out the omnipresent animal dung. Dropping the wooden bucket down into the well and drawing it back full, she upended the glorious cool cascade over her head, soaking her hair and her cotton gown. Standing there in the moonlight, she spread her arms and let the night air flow around her.

"How about another bucket for me?" Albert had crept up right behind her and put his hands on her still-small waist as he spoke. Lydia laughed and started to put the bucket into the well again but then realized Albert had other plans. "I've waited long enough, Lydia," he groaned in her ear. "I need my wife."

By Christmastime she was showing and Jacob Wilson McGee was born in April, the month General Lee surrendered at Appomattox. As she looked down into the solemn eyes of the child they would call Will, she prayed he would be her last. Although the war was over and it had not been as brutal in Kentucky as it was in other places, she had seen the changes in her neighbors and her family as they took sides on slavery. She did not believe there would be a real peace in her lifetime or that of her children. She wondered again about the little girl she had seen in the slave market in Louisville. Was she free now? Did she even live? If she did, how would the scars she bore ever heal?

NINE

TRUTH

LYDIA FINALLY SETTLED herself and baby Will comfortably in the front seat of the wagon and looked up for Joe and George. Her normally soft, even tones rose to a crescendo. "Joe! Get your brother away from that animal, and both of you get on this wagon!" She regretted the harsh words as soon as they escaped her lips. Albert never had to raise his voice to the boys or to her, but she had learned to read his stony silences like the phases of the moon. Baby Will, bored with nursing, entertained himself trying to unravel the fringed end of her scarf. Joe, so solemn and responsible, sometimes bore the brunt of her impatience; it was easy to forget he was only six.

"George!" shouted Joe as he pulled on his obsessed little brother's shirt. "Come on, we're going to town!" Lydia watched as he pulled her inquisitive second son away from the wet nose of the new spring lamb that had stuck a curious head through the fence slots. They both ran breakneck and pulled themselves up into the back of the wagon as their Pa emerged from the barn and slid into the driver's seat.

"Gee up," rang Albert's longest speech of the morning. The

cool, damp air held the words tight, but the mules responded quickly to the flick of Albert's whip and pulsed forward. The necessary trip to town for supplies was long overdue, but Albert would not start off until the last of the ewes had foaled. George started chattering immediately about the new one Albert had fetched into the pen last evening. Everyone ignored the boy's patter until he said, "I'm going to name him Will after my baby brother."

"No, George," Joe retorted quickly. "We don't name the livestock." Lydia had kept George in the house last spring when Pa had picked up one of the frolicking lambs, taken it to the back of the barn, and cut its throat quickly with his hunting knife. Farm children must come to terms early with the reality of life and death. The lamb was food like the eggs the chickens guarded, like the pig that provided sausage and ham and bacon for the family all winter. A tenderhearted child had to learn that difficult lesson quickly, and Joe felt responsible for educating his little brother.

Lydia glanced back at George, but Joe already had his hand on his brother's leg combined with a look of caution that made it clear that further talk on this subject would be dangerous. Lydia glanced over at Albert whose gaze never wavered from the rutted roadway. In the silence between them she thought of that hazy May morning nine years ago when they had driven away from the church in this same wagon. The handsome Albert had been all smiles as the ribbons that fluttered in her hair brushed against his cheek. Even then it had certainly not been the marriage she dreamed of or the life she had hoped for, but she had told herself that Albert loved her and that in time her feelings would grow. What had grown in her was not love or even affection but an increasing resentment of his disrespect for her and a deep sorrow for the life she would never have.

The life she imagined long ago before Jesse and Duncan died was so different from the one she was living. Her anger had gradually diminished, leaving her with an unrelenting sadness invisible to all around her save her brother Josiah and her friend Beth. They had both tried many avenues to bring back the Lydia they had once known, yet to no avail. Lydia found if she just kept going through the motions of living, she could almost forget the parts of her that were lost.

She watched Will's tiny lips as he made the motions of nursing although his mouth had long since slipped off her nipple as his eyes closed. She felt the weight of little George's body resting heavy against her back and heard Joe's soft lisping song that repeated the same phrase over and over. Her love for the children washed over her, making the feeling that her very life was slipping away almost bearable. The boys were quiet in anticipation of their rare adventure, and the unaccustomed inactivity soon made Lydia's eyelids feel heavy. The hour trip to Beaver Dam would take a bit longer with the recent rains. The normally dry creek bottoms would likely be flooded. The noise of the wagon faded into a familiar rocking cadence . . .

Lydia woke with a scream stuck in her throat and Joseph's hand shaking her shoulder.

"You were talking, Mama. You told Pa to save us, but we're okay." Adrenaline was coursing through her blood so fast that she almost lost her balance on the now-still wagon as she unfroze from her dream state. Instead of the whirling water of her dream, the dusty main street of Beaver Dam stretched before her.

"I'm sorry, Joe. I had a bad dream that we all fell in the creek." Lydia forced a smile to reassure the children. Joe and George laughed.

"You know I can swim, Mama. Why would that be a bad dream?" George giggled. "I would love to fall in the creek!"

"Yes, of course, my big boy. What a silly dream that was!"

Lydia held herself in check as everyone got down out of the wagon. "I'm going to clean up the baby. You boys go with your father to the mercantile, and best you behave."

Joe stage-whispered to George, "Or you won't get a peppermint stick." Two little gentlemen trailed off behind their father, leaving Lydia alone with her thoughts.

SHE STILL FELT the swirling water around her and her body being pulled roughly along in one whirlpool after another, always coming closer to the edge of the dam. Her arms flailed about frantically searching for her babies, and she screamed between gulps of cold silt-filled water for Albert to save them. She was sure they were further downstream, so ignoring her own safety, she let the river take her, hoping to catch up with one of them. Looking forward, she could see where the river seemed to stop only a few hundred feet ahead and still no child in sight. Just as the current sucked her under for the last drop over the edge of a waterfall, she looked up and saw them standing on the shore. Everyone was dry and nicely dressed as if they were going to get their portrait made. Albert held the baby while Joe and George held onto his pants leg with a look of horror on their little faces as they stared at their mother going over the abyss. Albert's handsome face just stared straight ahead as if he didn't see her, like he was just out for an afternoon walk. The last scream out of her throat had almost been audible. "Albert, please, please . . . help me!"

Lydia shook it off. "It was only a dream," she said, right out loud. She glanced up quickly to make sure no one was nearby to hear her. The streets seemed quiet for now. The train was due before long and with it the new harrow Albert had ordered. She tried to get her mind off the vivid pictures in her head by focusing on the supplies she needed at the store. Lydia went over her list again: yard goods to make new clothes for the boys, flour, coffee, sugar.

"Mama!" came a happy shout from George. She looked up to

see them running toward the wagon, shirttails flying. "Please, can you take us over to meet the train?" Albert was nowhere in sight.

"Where's your pa?"

"He's talking to some men at the store, but, Mama, the train will be here in no time. We want to be up front to watch. Papa said he was busy and to ask you. Please, Mama?"

One look at the hound-dog expression on both their faces and the insistent wail from George—"Train, Mama, train!"—convinced Lydia it was useless to protest. Besides, she would rather like to see the train arrive too. Perhaps she would catch a glance at the fine ladies sitting in the Pullman cars with their beautiful bonnets and silk dresses.

"Alright, boys, Joe, you hold George's hand and stay right there," she said. She put the baby down on the wagon seat and slid her feet over the side. Once she was steady, she gathered up the baby in her arms and set her face toward the depot. The boys took this as their clue and trotted ahead quickly. The sun had burned off the morning chill, but the day still held the sweet coolness of early spring. She tried to adjust her bonnet while holding the baby with one arm. The wind caught it as she passed the last building on Main Street, nearly pulling it off her head. Looking up, she saw the boys were almost to the depot. She thought of calling them but instead hurried her step to catch them before they reached the track.

The endless deafening thunder of the train was punctuated by the even louder scream of the steam engine's whistle. Hands linked, Joe and George were standing with their bare toes hanging over the edge of the platform as she arrived. "Boys! Step back!" she commanded, grabbing George's hand in hers and pulling him away from the edge. A small group of women in widow's weeds tossed a disapproving look her way, then turned to whisper among themselves. The boys obeyed reluctantly but strained their necks forward as far as possible as the whistle shrieked a second time. The baby tensed in her arms at the explosive sounds and smells of the slowing train. Joe and George stood fascinated as the enormous engine creeped by in front of them, bells clanging, metal wheels groaning with impatience. As a hiss of steam and acrid smoke suddenly let loose, little George took refuge behind his mother's skirt. The monstrous engine finally slid by them and stopped with a jerk several hundred yards down the tracks.

Lydia felt the collective breath of the watcher's release as passenger doors scraped open. Hoping for a glimpse of the ladies in the Pullman car, she walked a few hundred feet down the dusty path, George still holding onto her skirt. The train would not be moving until it filled up with water and coal, so she had plenty of time. After months on the farm, being around so many strangers made her feel slightly claustrophobic. She navigated as deftly as possible with babe in arms and another pulling on her apron. The platform was clogged with those in the midst of coming and going, tradespeople, the rail staff, and a few other curious gawkers. The passenger car was just ahead, and the space between the throng and the car had just enough room for her to fit if she hurried. Pressing forward quickly, she ran full force into a man getting off the train, causing him to drop his carpetbag and the smart derby hat he was wearing.

"Oh! So sorry, sir! Let me help you." Lydia quickly let go of George's hand, scooped up the hat, and extended it to the nattily dressed gentleman.

"No harm done, missus. I should watch where I'm going." With the keen eyes of a salesman he took in Lydia's flushed face. It was angelic, yet somehow erotic, with crystal-clear green eyes, pale-peach skin, and a sprinkling of freckles on her cheeks. Her home-spun calico bonnet was sitting askew on her head, the soft familiar auburn hair struggling to stay pinned. He gazed transfixed at her for a few seconds too long. Then he took the proffered hat from her and managed to speak despite the lump he felt in his throat. He touched his hand to the broad black hat, marshaled his facial expression, and said, "Hello, Lydia. This is certainly unexpected."

Lydia felt the world spin around her as she looked into the clear hazel eyes of Duncan Porter. Somehow she regained the use of her mouth just as he was turning to go. "But it can't be. You are dead and buried these nine years at least."

"You have been misinformed, my dear. I must have written you thirty letters those first three years after I left, but when I never heard back from you, I assumed you had made other choices."

Lydia stammered and shook her head. "What are you talking about? I never got one letter from you!"

George's tug at her skirt pulled her back to reality. "Mama, I want to go on the train like Joe." He pointed up to the window where her eldest was pressing his face.

"Joe!" Lydia gasped, mortified. "Get off this instant!" Her shout was not loud enough for Joe to hear over the noise on the platform, but the look on her face made the young miscreant scramble for the door. In a few seconds both boys were standing shamefaced beside her and Duncan was gone. She scolded Joe over his protests of innocence, not too harshly, however, as she was still reeling from the sight of the man she first thought was a ghost.

"Boys," lectured Lydia, "I understand how exciting it is to see the train and want to ride on it, but the conductor won't stand for a couple of wild little barefoot Indians running down the aisles disturbing the paying passengers."

"Can we be pass-a-gers, Mama?" said George. "I wanna ride the train."

She heard a laugh and looked up to see Duncan's now smiling eyes on her again, this time with a large trunk sitting beside him. "Tell me, boys, what big city would you like to visit and what do you want to do there?"

"Louisville," George said immediately.

Joe shook his head. "No, George, we should go all the way to Chicago."

"Chicago!" said the stranger. "Good choice. Not that Louisville isn't nice, but nothing compares to the Windy City. You boys want to hear all about it? I live in Chicago when I'm not on the road." They gazed up at him with eagerness and responded with a polite but loud "Yes, sir!"

Lydia's head was already shaking as she said, "That's very generous of you, Mr. Porter, but the children have done enough damage for one day. You've seen the train, boys. I know your father expects your help packing the supplies in the wagon." Just the mention of their dad turned the excitement in their little faces to a more sober countenance.

"Let's go," Lydia said, wrangling the reluctant little ones down the dusty path that led from the depot to Main Street. In truth she really wanted to talk longer to Duncan, but she could not allow the boys to be so familiar with a man they did not know. The boys continued to protest with "But, Mommy, why?" until Lydia spoke sharply to them again. "Because your father will be waiting for us. Now, look where you're going, boys."

DUNCAN MULLED OVER the accidental meeting with the beautiful Lydia who had promised to write to him and to wait for his return. At first he had written weekly, but as months went by and he never heard back from her, his letters slowed and then he stopped altogether. He had grieved the loss of her every day since, and now it seemed someone had sown lies to keep them apart. Duncan hefted his trunk and headed over to make the rounds of the general stores on Main Street to take orders for Christmas merchandise.

Duncan saw Mr. Austin standing behind the counter, deep in conversation with a familiar-looking customer. While he waited, he turned over memories in his mind. When a break came in the conversation, he spoke, "Albert McGee, as I live and breathe! How long has it been?"

Albert turned to face Duncan's extended hand, hesitating a bit too long before he spoke. It was very clear he knew exactly who stood before him and why he had hoped this moment would never come.

Finally the prosperous-looking man spoke. "I'm Duncan Porter, Albert, we were in school together many years ago. I was only thirteen and you were fifteen when we met, so you likely don't remember me."

Albert's face stayed frozen, but he finally extended his hand. "Well, certainly, Duncan, Duncan Porter. Your sister was the schoolmarm, and then both of you moved my last year. I believe she married if I'm not mistaken."

"Right, I was just a kid and didn't have a choice. Turned out to be a good thing. My sis picked a good man, and he helped me continue my education. Then I took a few years off to fight for the Federal Army when the war broke out."

"So, Duncan, you look like you're doing well. What brings you back to these parts?"

"Business, Albert. I'm a salesman for the Marshall Field's company out of Chicago. I'm here taking orders for Christmas goods."

Mr. Austin had been listening quietly. "That so, Mr. Porter? I was told to expect a Simon McAlister."

"So sorry, Mr. Austin, It seems I have arrived ahead of the sad news. Simon died from injuries he received at Chattanooga unfortunately. We fought with General Negley's division. I found Simon wounded and took him home hoping he would recover. We both planned to work for Field's after the war, but that was not to be. He lingered for a long time, but he finally gave up the fight about five months ago. I decided to take his advice about the job, however. It's a good life for a single man."

"So you never married?" Albert asked. "Would have expected a handsome fellow like you to have a wife and some children by now, Duncan."

"No, still hope to someday if I ever find the right girl. How about you, Albert? Married? Children?"

"Yes indeed, Duncan, married with three boys already."

Duncan flashed back to the meeting at the train and asked cautiously, "You and Lydia?"

"Right you are. I recall you were kind of sweet on her too."

Duncan could not help but notice that Albert was acting more than a little nervous. Just then Lydia came out of the back room carrying the baby and a bolt of material. The boys trailed along behind her.

"Lydia," Albert said with a guilty tone, "I'm almost done here. Get the boys back in the wagon, and I'll be there in a minute."

"I need a few more things, Albert. I have a list, remember?" Duncan turned toward her while they were talking, and Lydia exclaimed, "Isn't it wonderful, Albert? Duncan is still alive. Seems odd that Ma got that letter right before we started courting saying he passed away. Let me think, what was it? Typhoid, that's right. Perhaps your brother-in-law sent that letter out prematurely, Duncan?

Duncan looked puzzled. "What? When was this? Why would he say that I was . . ." Suddenly it dawned on him why Albert would be anxious.

"Give me the list and go wait in the wagon, Lydia." Albert used his no-back-talk voice, then softly added, "Boys, first one back in the wagon and ready to go gets two peppermint sticks!"

Lydia reluctantly handed Albert the list and followed the boys out. When Albert turned around, Duncan was gone. Out of Albert's sight he had headed to the back, slipped out the door, and ran to look for Lydia. He caught up to her just as she was ready to put the baby down on the seat. He whispered breathlessly, "I'll leave a letter for you with the PO at the store. Read it and please write back to me." He thrust a scrap of paper in her hand with his address written on it.

Lydia just nodded, and Duncan smiled, then turned and hurried back to the store. The sun was still shining on the wagon, on her children, and on Lydia's calico bonnet, but her field of vision had narrowed to a small dark circle. The noise of Albert dropping his purchases into the wagon startled Lydia back to her grim reality. All the long way home Lydia only spoke if one of the children was vying for her attention while uncharacteristically Albert chatted on about everything except the obvious fact that Duncan Porter was still alive and he had known it all along.

Late that night with supper finished and the children tucked in, Lydia and Albert lay unsleeping in their bed. She felt his hand reach over for her as if nothing had changed between them. In their years together Lydia had always been compliant to his advances, never analyzing if her response was out of duty, fear, or resignation. Albert did not demand enthusiasm and was certainly not concerned about her objections. Still, he did not seem surprised when she froze and pushed him away. It was at that moment that Lydia knew for certain he had been complicit in her parents' lie, but her heart still needed to hear the words from his mouth.

"Just tell me one thing, Albert, and I want the truth. Did you know?"

His nervous response confirmed everything. "Know what, Lydia? What are you talking about?"

Lydia rolled over and pretended to sleep. Albert dropped his advances and pretended to do the same. Toward the dawn of that long dark night both of them dozed off.

When the sun finally rose on a new day, Albert had no idea his marriage was over.

TEN

HELL HATH NO FURY

AFTER MORNING CHORES were done and Albert went to the barn, Lydia finally located the valise that held her old journals. It was tucked in the bottom of the cedar chest Pa had made for her when she was twelve. She turned to a blank page and wrote at the top:

October 20, 1868 – Today I start a new chapter in a life that has been based on lies.

She spent the next hour writing out her feelings as she had long ago when she still had dreams. It always helped her to focus her mind and make decisions. She was careful to hide the journal before Albert came in for dinner. By the time she finished writing, she had a plan and a purpose. Albert, seeing her going about her life as before, assured himself that Lydia's unhappiness was short-lived. He was even relieved that the secret was out and congratulated himself on how well he had managed everything.

Later that week he told Lydia he needed her to pack food for the next day, as he would take Joe with him to help his brothers cut timber for a new barn. He did not want to have to come home for midday. It was not an uncommon request, so the next morning when Lydia presented him with a basket, he gave her a quick peck on the cheek; then he and Joe went out, hitched the mules to the wagon, and set off for the day.

When he got home that evening, he was surprised to find the small buggy out of its usual place in the barn. He asked Lydia about it first thing when he went in the house, and she replied airily, "Oh, I took the boys to visit my parents today. It has been quite a while since they have had time with the children."

Albert looked carefully for signs that his wife was upset, but seeing nothing obvious to his eyes, he sat down to supper. "Next time let me know ahead. I don't like you going off alone with the boys. What if something happened to the horse or the buggy broke down? You could not manage alone."

Lydia gave him an undecipherable look. "Don't worry," she said. "I won't be going back again." Seeing his expression, Lydia added, "By myself, I mean." She smiled sweetly as if to take any sting out of the comment. If Albert had known his wife better, it would have been clear that a raging storm was brewing, but he was not a man who gave much thought to a woman's moodiness.

"Well, that's settled then. Good," Albert replied, unworried.

When she lay down to sleep that night, the horror of her mother's revelations looped over and over in her head. George had been happy with his grandpa in the barn, and the baby went to sleep in the old cradle by the stairs. Lydia's conversation with her mother had started tentatively.

"Ma, you'll never guess who I saw in town last week . . . Duncan Porter."

Her ma barely flinched, but Lydia knew her too well not to recognize the shock. Lydia continued, "He's doing really well, a salesman for Marshall Field's now, it seems, and he lives in Chicago." Ma still didn't say a word, just kept stirring the jam she was cooking on the stove. Lydia tried again, "I remember how much I longed to see Chicago when I was in school. At least I did get to visit Louisville with Uncle Jesse."

Finally Ma could take it no longer. "That fool old man! I just thank God he died before you turned eighteen. When I think about how you might have spent that money . . ." Ma stopped midsentence realizing what she had just admitted.

"What money, Ma?" Lydia's reply was icy.

Ma's reaction to being caught in the deception was predictable. She moved the jam to the back of the stove to keep it warm, wiped her hands on her apron, and turned to face Lydia, shameless.

"You would have run off to that school and come home ruined instead of marrying someone steady and dependable like Albert. That money meant you were able to start off your life with a nice home and a barn instead of struggling for years like we did."

Lydia just stared at the stranger speaking from behind her mother's eyes. When she finally was able to reply, the voice her mother heard was just as alien.

"Everything you told me after Jesse died was a lie. You let me think he broke his promise to me, and you kept me from everything I loved, including Duncan Porter! You knew he was alive, didn't you?" The puzzle pieces kept falling into place. "My lord, Ma, you took my letter, you read it, and you manufactured the letter saying he was dead. You also read and destroyed all the other letters I wrote to him and all the ones he sent to me." Shaking with anger and realizing her legs would no longer hold her, Lydia sank into the kitchen chair. Ma took her silence as calm and started trying to reason with her.

"Now, Lydia, you know we only did what was best for you. Pa and I didn't want you moving so far away, especially with the unrest in the country at that time. We knew you'd be safest with Albert.

We really never knew anything much about that Porter boy, and he had no family to speak of and no prospects. Look at all you have now, Lydia, your home, your boys, a good, God-fearing husband. You know if you had that money in hand, it would have been gone in six months and you'd be back here without a pot to piss in. Albert was wise to tell us you intended to run off with that boy."

Lydia gasped. "So let me get this clear. You took the money Uncle Jesse left me and you gave it to Albert. You never mailed any of the letters I handed to Pa to post to Duncan, you destroyed the ones he sent to me, and finally you and Papa and Albert conspired to make me believe Duncan was dead. Does that cover it all? Is there anything I'm leaving out?" Lydia paused waiting for an answer from Ma. After long moments of silence she added, "Perhaps you poisoned Uncle Jesse to help him move on to his reward a bit quicker?"

"Lydia!" screeched Ma. "That's a horrible thing to say. You think I would murder Jesse?"

"I don't really know, Ma. I would never have thought you capable of all the rest, but I do not hear a denial of anything except murder. It's good to know you have some limits."

Lydia gathered up the baby and her things and headed for the door. "Good-bye, Ma. I don't expect to ever see you again in this life or the next."

Ma scowled and spit like she was the one who had been harmed. "Why are you always so dramatic, Lydia? I'm sure your Pa and your husband will have something to say about that."

Lydia was already out of the door headed to the barn and her carriage. Pa had fed the mare, and George was helping by tossing hay down from high in the loft. "Come on down here, George. We're headed home." Lydia then turned to her pa and spoke in a softer voice. "I just want to know one thing. Is all of the money Jesse left me gone?"

Pa's face fell. He did not even try to deny but proceeded to make it worse.

"I so wanted to tell you, Lydia, but Ma convinced me we were doing the right thing. Now that you're happily married and have the boys, you can surely see that it was for the best." Then he added sheepishly, "There was only a tiny bit left after the house, the barn, your new clothes, the livestock. Ma needed a few things after you were gone. I'm afraid we spent it all, Lydia."

She feared even to ask her last question, but she had to find out. "Did Josiah know, Pa? Was he in on it too?"

"No, Lydia, no. We didn't tell him a thing." Pa hung his head further. "We knew he would tell you and we just wanted to protect you. Ma said you'd thank us later, if you ever found out."

Lydia stared at her father and recalled the only time he had ever raised his hand against her was for a childish lie she once told about playing in the barn loft in her Sunday clothes. She cursed the tears that rolled down her cheeks thinking that Pa might see them as sorrow. While she felt sorrow, it was down deep under an anger more profound than any she had ever experienced in her life.

"You were wrong, Pa. Thankfulness is the furthest thing from my mind. I will never forgive you or Ma for what you've done to me." Seeing the surprise on his face, she added, "Do you remember that time you spanked me when I lied to you about playing in the barn loft, Pa? I was five years old and I've never forgotten it. Have you given any thought as to what your punishment might be on judgment day?"

George had clamored into the buggy by now. Lydia handed the baby to George and climbed in beside him. She took one long farewell look at her Pa standing there in dirty overhauls and tattered flannel shirt. Why had she not noticed all the creases in his tanned face before or how much gray was sprinkled through his once black hair? The sorrow and rage and pity that churned up in her stomach was unlike any emotion she had ever felt. "Bye, Pa," she said, just

loud enough for him to hear. George echoed her good-byes cheer-
fully as they drove off toward home.

The week that followed was unnaturally calm. Sunday morning
Lydia was up by sunrise and made breakfast while Albert tended the
animals. She had dressed herself and all the children for church
while Albert lingered over breakfast. After having sat on the hard
wooden bench staring at the face of the preacher for what seemed
like hours, she could not remember a word of the sermon. Albert
thought nothing of it when she spent some time chatting with her
best friend, Beth, afterward. Lydia had already prepared her first lie
for Albert if he had seen her slipping the letter for Duncan into her
friend's hand. She repeated it to herself, "Recipe for plum tarts," but
she did not need to use it this time. She would save that lie for
another day.

It was almost three weeks before Beth pulled her aside at church
and slipped the letter into her hand. She had to wait until Albert left
the house Monday to read.

April 16, 1867

My dearest Lydia,

*The letter you wrote to me arrived this morning. To think that
all these years I have mourned your loss from my life only to find
out that you mourned what you believed to be my death. It is
indescribably cruel of your parents and Albert to conspire to make
you believe me indifferent, much less dead. To do that and then to
withhold Jesse's inheritance from you and keep you from following
your dreams is beyond forgiveness. I am glad your father at least
felt a bit ashamed, but I never thought him such a coward as to go
along with your mother and defraud you. I have friends who are
lawyers and we could sue them, but since you know the money
was spent on the house Albert built, there would be little point. I
do believe you could obtain a divorce, possibly in Indiana,
although it would be a scandal and it seems it is always the*

woman who bears the shame. The children would most likely be
lost to you regardless, unless Albert would let them go willingly.

I wish the reality of your situation were more promising. I
believe the best we can hope for is for you to escape. From your
letter it seems your relationship with Albert is not a warm and
loving one. If you are willing to leave him and come away with
me, I can offer you a new and better life here in Chicago. I am
aware this offer is not made out of altruism but from my selfish
need for you. Since I have never married and have means of my
own to support us, I make this offer to you with all my heart. I
need you to think long and carefully about this as to do so you
would lose everything you now have. I promise I will live my life
trying to make it up to you. I know it may be hard to trust me now
when so many have betrayed you, but truly, Lydia, you are the
only woman I have ever loved, and if you give me the chance, I
will prove my feelings for you.

Yours eternally,
Duncan

Lydia read the letter over a dozen times running through the
gamut of emotions she felt during each repeat. Words from the letter
raced through her head like a mantra: love, scandal, escape, and
always ending with children. Her reply to him was as contradictory
as her emotions.

My dear Duncan,

I am so torn by your offer. I fear the life you suggest would
ruin us both, and the thought of losing my children leaves me
numb and cold inside. I have to ask myself if it would hurt them
more for me to leave them or to stay here growing more bitter
each day? No matter the crime my parents and Albert have
committed, the children are innocent.

For all of Albert's faults he is a good father, especially for our firstborn, Joe. The two of them are so much alike I believe he would be over my loss in a short time. George is like me, like my brother Josiah. He would grieve and his father would have no patience for it. I would just have to pray that he would cling to his brother and they would find a way through together. Baby Jacob is still a mystery, but he seems more like Joe than George.

When I recall our final kiss before you left and the promises we made, my soul swells up with longing. Am I a fool for not rushing toward the sweetness of what we had? I am not the young girl you left standing, crying outside the churchyard, and you are not the fourteen-year-old boy who courted me so shyly. Can love like we felt be lost? When I saw you at the train, I knew the answer, but now, back in this life of compromises, I cannot imagine actually leaving. Then the anger of the lies flares up in me again and I cannot imagine staying.

I have not really confronted Albert about his deception like I did my parents, but he knows something is very wrong. Soon I know he will visit with them and we will have to have a reckoning. Pray for me, Duncan, because I know it will not go well.

I must stop now as Albert will be home soon. When you write again, please tell me more about your life in Chicago. I try to imagine what the city must be like, but the only thing I have to compare it to is Louisville and that was years ago. If I came, where would we live? What would you tell your sister about our situation? I am not making any promises about coming, you understand. I just need to know what to expect if I should.

With deepest affection,

Lydia

When Albert came home, Lydia had supper ready and the children were quiet and busy. It seemed that he was looking for something to be off so he could complain when his eyes fell on the journal she had forgotten to put away. "What is this?" His hand was almost on the book when she snatched it.

"Just some stories I am writing," Lydia replied.

"I like a good story. Let me see," Albert demanded, although she had not seen him pick up more than a newspaper since he graduated high school.

"You would find these boring, just things about my day, like food I make, laundry, things the children are doing. Nothing that would interest you." Lydia tucked the book quickly into her apron and went to fetch the stew from the stove. "Come to the table, everyone, supper is ready."

Albert did not press further, but it was clear he would not rest easy until he had read her journal. His reading would have meant the end of them, but she was past the end already. The card she still held was the element of surprise. She wanted to keep her plans to herself for as long as possible. By writing, Lydia gave her anger a voice, and the power within her grew like some magical spell was being cast with her words. Looking back, she realized her life had never recovered from the darkness that started when Uncle Jesse died. When her mother had finally admitted the conspiracy to deceive, it was as if scales had fallen from her eyes. Seen in the glaring light of truth, Albert's professed need for her felt a lot more like possession than love, his deep concern merely a need to establish ownership and control. He condemned himself daily with every look and action.

It was hard to keep the letters from Duncan secret. Sometimes it seemed she was trying to be caught, especially so because with each letter the distance between Albert and herself widened. The contrast between the deep connection and communication she and Duncan shared and the shallowness and boredom of the hours she spent with Albert grew more striking with each passing week. She was grateful when Josiah came for a visit one day when Albert was out. The first thing he said to her was, "I'm so sorry, Lydia." Cleary he had spoken to their parents. Tears came to both their eyes as they hugged. Long minutes later Lydia pulled back and composed herself.

"You knew no more than I did, Josiah, and you were even younger than I was at the time. You have nothing to be sorry about."

"But if I had only known—" Josiah started but Lydia stopped him.

"There was nothing you could have done, my dear brother. I know you would have moved heaven and earth for me if it had been possible. Ma and Pa made the decision for me, and since I was not of age and a woman, nothing stood in their way. The pain of it eats at me every minute. I cannot bear to see Ma and Pa again, and the bitterness of it all is destroying what little affection I may have had for Albert. I cannot stay here, Josiah. I simply cannot." For the first time since she learned of the deceit, Lydia broke down sobbing.

Josiah held her again. "I know it's so hard, but there is no real choice. You are Albert's wife, the children—"

Lydia stopped him. "I do have a choice, Josiah." She paused while her brother looked at her perplexed. "Duncan and I have been in contact. He is alive and prosperous. He wants me to come to Chicago and start a new life."

Josiah drew back like he had been snakebit. "Lydia, no! How could you even consider it? You cannot take the boys along, and they are so young."

"The boys are the only reason I have not already left," Lydia admitted. I've thought of little else. For all his faults, Albert is a good father. Perhaps a bit stern and businesslike, but the boys don't seem to be bothered by that. If I left, and mind you, I am not certain I will, I could write to them and maybe see them sometimes. Joe can read now and George is learning his letters. I know you and Mary would look over them too; plus, their grandparents are all nearby." This was the first time Lydia had been able to speak her justifications out loud. They did not sound as rational when she heard herself say them as they had when she put them on paper in her letters to Duncan.

"Just promise me this, Lydia. Make no move until you've talked to me again. I need to think about this and so do you. Promise me."

"I promise, Josiah. I won't go without letting you know." It was a promise she could not keep.

ELEVEN

ESCAPE

BETH HAD SLIPPED the letter into her pocket at church yesterday, but Lydia had to wait until Albert was out of the house this morning before she could read it. She was not sure if he lingered longer than usual or if it was her anxiety that made the time pass so slowly, but finally his horse crested the hill and he was gone. She tore the letter open and read:

> *March 31, 1869*
>
> *My dearest Lydia,*
>
> *The news of the conflict with Albert makes my heart ache for you and the children. You cannot delay leaving any longer. I will be on my way to get you as soon as I post this letter. You can expect me no later than the twenty-first of April. I will bring a buggy and camp for a few days at the crossroads where you turn to reach your farm.*

Lydia let the letter fall to the table. Could it finally be happening? The reality of actually leaving was only slightly less terrifying than the idea of staying. The last few months since she had known the truth had been grim. Her excuses to Albert for not visiting her parents during the long winter months finally caused him to go talk to them himself a month ago. His face was ashen when he returned, but they did not speak about it until the children were in bed that night.

"Why did you not tell me that you argued with your parents?" Albert's blue eyes were accusing and angry, but he kept his voice under control.

"Why did you not tell me you conspired with them to steal my inheritance and keep me from my dreams of going to school and marrying Duncan?" Lydia's reply had been waiting on her tongue for months now, but when spoken they seemed to explode like a sudden impulse.

Albert's voice stayed even and condescending. "You never knew what was best for you, Lydia. We had to protect you from all those ridiculous notions and scoundrels that would take advantage of you."

"Scoundrels! You mean someone who would steal money, dreams, and the maidenhood of a young girl? Who does that sound like, Albert?" Lydia's voice was soft but chilling.

Albert just stared at her with the look of a man caught with his hand in the till. His tone changed. "Now, Lydia, no need to get hysterical. Nothing was taken from you by force. You have this fine house, three strong sons, and I don't interfere with all that infernal writing you do." With an astounding lack of awareness of Lydia's pain, Albert's arm was suddenly around her waist, pulling her to him. "And you know you offered up your body to me willingly." His mouth was suddenly on hers and his hands pulling up her gown.

He was startled with how much force was in her small body. Lydia pushed him away with a restrained hiss of "No!" Albert had a look of total surprise on his face. "How could you possibly think we could fix this in bed, Albert McGee? You raped and shamed me on our wedding night. After that I was too afraid of you to ever object.

You have no idea how many nights I have cried myself to sleep listening to you snore. I am not afraid of you now, Albert. As far as I'm concerned, that part of our life is over."

"I am your husband, Lydia. You just aren't thinking clearly right now. You'll be over this in a few days."

Lydia stared at him in shock. She spoke only with her eyes as she walked over to the tiny settee in the bedroom, just big enough for one small person to curl up. She turned her back to him and pulled the throw up to her chin. Albert hated his feeling of helplessness, but not ever having known Lydia to be this angry, he decided tomorrow would be time enough to deal with it. Cooler heads would prevail, of that he was sure.

Lydia shivered as she shook off the memory of that dark night and the shadows of the days that followed. She picked up Duncan's letter from the table and continued to read . . .

You remember the little grove of trees and the spring that sits off the road there? I will wait there until you can slip away. Do not try and bring too much. I will buy you whatever you need once we get to Chicago. Be very careful, my darling.

It was already April 19, so Duncan must be very near. Her heart leaped at the thought and then the dread sank in of all that must be done before she left. Before the packing or even the thought of what to take, she had to deal with what she must leave behind. She could not talk to her son Joe beforehand for fear he would tell Albert, but she could write him a letter explaining things in terms she hoped he would understand. She would write one for each of the boys and one for Albert. Then there was her dear brother Josiah. She had promised to tell him before she left, but how could she do it with only these few days left? It would not be possible, but she would post him a letter from the road. She would try her best to make him understand. She hated to leave him with the task of telling her parents and brother because she was sure they would find a way to blame him.

It was the morning of April 21, 1869, when Albert found the packet of letters tucked under a food-filled basket on the roughly built oak table in the kitchen. He had already called for Lydia a number of times without any response. While he was not a man given to refined feelings, he sensed something was very off this morning, but still he did not attempt to read the letters. Instead, he peered into the covered basket and discovered bread, boiled eggs, butter, and a jar of jam. To avoid the letters he turned to the wood-stove and started stirring up the coals and reloading it with logs. He picked up the iron kettle and found it already filled with water, so he left it on the stove while he got the tea, plates, and cups off the shelf. Only then did he sit down to open the first sheet of paper, the one that bore his name in Lydia's delicate hand.

Albert,

By the time you read this, I'll be many miles away. You know things have not been right between us for many months now, perhaps they never were. I have given it long thought, and I find I cannot live with the injustice done to me by you and my parents any longer. I will miss the children more than I can say, but I know I cannot take them from you, and in truth I could not take them with me in my present circumstances. I will write to you when I am settled and let you know where I am. I know the children will have many questions, which is why I have written them each a letter. Joe will be able to read his by himself, but you will have to help George. Save the one for Will until he is older.

I think it probably best if you file for divorce. I know it is a drastic thing, but it is becoming more common and I know you will need a helpmate now that I am gone. I only ask that you pick someone who is kind to the boys, makes sure they get help with school, and will not raise them with a heavy hand.

One more thing, Albert. I hope that you pick someone who will make you happy. In all the years we have been together, we have never used the word love between us. I have always felt more like a possession to you than a lover, more a housekeeper than a partner. If you could have once found it in your heart to say the words I love you, *perhaps I would have tried to stick it out despite my anger over the way we started. Even all those times when you took my body with what appeared to be passion, not once did the word* love *find its way to your mouth. I know you will not believe it right now, but even though our marriage had a rocky start, I did come to care for you and I tried to be a good wife. I believe if you had met me halfway, we could have learned to love each other. Perhaps someday you may find it in your heart to forgive me, but if not, please do not make the boys suffer because of your anger.*

Sincerely

Lydia

Albert went through the rest of the letters and read them over briefly. When he heard the boy's footfall from upstairs, he folded them all and tucked them into his shirt pocket. Rising, he pulled the now boiling kettle off the stove and poured it over the tea leaves he had put in the pot earlier. As the boys came scampering down the stairs, he portioned out the food Lydia had left for them. "Pa," asked Joe, "where is Ma?"

"Eat now, we can talk about that later," his father replied. The three exchanged glances around the table. Will's little mouth started to open, but Joe, sensing something was up, poked him under the table. When Will met his eyes with reproach, he again started to speak, but seeing his brother's stern look, he sat silent as he had learned to do when they were hunting with Pa. The meal was quickly over as no one had much of an appetite.

"Get dressed and meet me in the barn," Pa ordered. The younger boys whispered between themselves after they got to their room, but bowed to Joe's demand that they all stay quiet around Pa.

In the barn they all pitched in as they were able and tended the animals. There was no milk today as their only producer was due to drop a calf any day. When they were done, Pa hitched up the wagon and pulled it outside. "Hop on, boys. We're headed over to Grandma and Grandpa McGee's."

The boys clambered aboard excited. "Do you think Grandma will have a treat for us?" asked George.

"She just might," Pa said, knowing his mother was never without something for unexpected company or grandchildren.

"Maybe molasses cookies," said Joe.

"Or spice cake," said George.

"Peppermint sticks!" shouted John, who was a big fan of the store-bought treat.

Their surprise turned out to be fried apple pies left over from last night's supper. Even though they had finished breakfast a bit more than two hours before, they tucked in without hesitation, barely noticing their pa taking Grandmother aside to whisper to her. Then Grandma went to the springhouse and came back with a pitcher of chilled milk. The boys were stunned and a bit suspicious of their unusual midweek treat. Pa had slipped away to the barn and returned with his father. The boys came running to their grandpa for hugs.

"Well, boys, how would you like to come help me in the barn a bit, and then we can head down to the creek and catch something for supper tonight?" All three heads nodded with enthusiasm.

Joe began to sense a setup. "Is it okay for us to go fishing, Pa?"

Albert acted like he was thinking it over. Then he kneeled down on his heels to look Joe in the eye. "Yes, it certainly is. In fact, Grandma and Grandpa would like for you to spend a few days with them. I have a few of your things in the wagon, and I can fetch you on Saturday."

Not wanting to break whatever spell was making their day so perfect, the boys just turned to each other in wonder and then followed their grandpa out to the barn with yells of glee. After they were gone, Albert sat down at the table with his mother, tears in his eyes. "I don't know what to do next, Ma. How am I going to manage without her? I would go after her, but I don't think I could get her to come home."

"Why would you want her to come home, Albert?" His mother could barely suppress her anger when she spoke. "She ran off and left you with the children sleeping in their beds. Poor little angels. What kind of mother would do a thing like that? You know I always felt like she had too many notions to be a good wife to you. If you want my advice, you should divorce her and forget about her. We can keep the boys as long as you need us to."

"You may be right, Ma. I need to think. If I can find a house-keeper, I'll pick up the boys on Saturday like I said. They need to be back to their own beds soon. I'll see you then." Then he rose, hugged his mom, and headed out the door.

IN THE NEXT few days Albert's grief became anger. He stopped by the home of the Renfrow family Friday morning. They were distantly related on his mother's side and had several daughters who were attractive, one whose betrothed had been killed in the war. As he rode up to the house, he saw her hanging sheets in the yard. He tied up the team and headed to the front porch to greet the family but not without giving notice to the graceful movements of the slim dark-haired woman. He waved at her as he passed, and she nodded her head in response. Her mother heard him coming and had stepped out on the porch. "Well, I do say, Albert McGee! What a wonderful surprise. Come in, come in."

"Roxanna!" Mrs. Renfrow shouted to the woman in the yard.

"Fetch your pa from the barn. Albert, can I get you something to drink? Looks like you've had a thirsty ride."

"Thank you, Mrs. Renfrow. A glass of water would be much appreciated."

Mr. Renfrow came into the house followed by Roxanna. He was as cordial as his wife and greeted Albert warmly. Albert found himself continuing to glance at their daughter's shy smile while Mr. and Mrs. Renfrow looked at him expectantly.

Albert had practiced his speech all the way over in the buggy, but the words were not coming easily now that he was facing real people instead of the haunches of his big chestnut mare.

"I need you to keep everything I'm going to tell you secret for now." Everyone at the table leaned in with their eyes wide when they heard Albert's startling opening gambit. "Lydia has left me. When I woke this morning, my babes were in their beds and their mother had left me a note saying she was gone and was not coming back."

The Renfrows' horrified faces made it clear that his announcement had made the desired impact. Roxanne's hand went over her mouth as if she was expecting her breakfast to come back up. Mrs. Renfrow leaped out of her seat and put her arm around Albert's shoulder, patting him on the back. Mr. Renfrow's face went dark. He was the first to speak. "What can we do to help, Albert? What do you need?"

Albert was the picture of despair. "I need my wife back, Mr. Renfrow, but that's never going to happen." He kept his eyes focused on John Renfrow, avoiding looking at the wrenching empathy on Roxanna's face. "Since that is impossible, I simply need someone to come tend to my motherless children so I can run the farm."

"Please let me help, Albert," Roxanna blurted out.

Her parents both looked at her slightly startled. Albert's look was briefly triumphant, then quickly snapped to shamefaced.

"Oh no, I couldn't ask that of you, Roxanna. You're a single woman. I was just hoping your family might know someone who could help. I didn't mean to imply . . ." Albert stammered.

Mr. Renfrow said quickly, "No, Roxanne, we cannot risk your reputation. Absolutely not."

Then Mrs. Renfrow spoke up firm but strong. "Albert, I think we can work something out. Roxanna has three younger sisters here at home. Roxanna can bring Fran with her. They can both come home on Saturday night, and then you can pick them up at church on Sunday to travel back to your place. It will all be completely aboveboard."

All of them stared at her openmouthed. Albert practically held his breath waiting for Mr. Renfrow to speak.

"Well . . .yes," he said slowly. "Now, Mama, are you sure you can manage the house without two of the girls here?"

"Pish, of course. Fran is a daydreamer anyway. I spend much of my day getting her to do her chores. The responsibility of helping with the little ones will do her a world of good. Of course, with all her energy Roxanna is an enormous help, but Effie and Laura can step up and do more. Knowing that their older sister will pick up their slack has probably not been good for them."

At this point Roxanne's eyes were dancing with excitement. She was five years younger than Albert, but she remembered admiring him from afar in school. Her older sister, Rachel, had vied for his attention, but he never had eyes for anyone but Lydia. Rachel had ended up marrying a Union officer who came though during the war, and now she was living happily in Ohio. After Roxanna lost her sweetheart, Luke, during the war, she had thought to be a spinster forever. She could not believe this stroke of luck. Of course, she could not marry him right away, but he would have no choice but to file for divorce from Lydia after she had deserted him.

"Roxanna?" Ma must have been speaking for some time while she was daydreaming.

"Yes, Ma?"

"Why don't you go pack a bag for you and for Fran. Send her to me and I will explain what is going on. Albert, do you want to wait for her or shall we bring her over later?"

And so it was done. An hour later Roxanne and Fran were tucked into the buggy with their belongings in a carpetbag headed for Alberts's house. When he brought the boys home on Saturday, the house was clean and tidy with every shelf rearranged. Supper was on the table when they came in the door: chicken and dumplings, green beans, and the first of the strawberries from the garden for dessert. Everything looked perfect. Albert and the Renfrow girls were all smiles. The boys, however, were holding back tears all evening and picked at their food during supper. Albert prodded them about their manners and reminded them that Roxanne and Fran were not strangers since they saw them every Sunday.

Joe's bright blue eyes were clouded with tears when he spoke. "Thank you for making us this great supper, Miss Renfrow. I guess I filled up on treats at Grandma's house. I'm just not very hungry. George and Will nodded in agreement with their brother. Roxanne cleaned up the kitchen in record time and then scurried the boys up the steps to bed. Her instinct to help these motherless boys bubbled up as she tucked Joe into bed.

"I just want you to know I'm not going to try to replace your mother, Joe. I know you must miss her so much." Joe started sobbing. He let Roxanna gather him into her arms, and she held him for a long time.

Finally he said though his sobs, "Do you know how she died? Pa wouldn't tell me."

Roxanna caught her breath and stammered, "Died? Your pa told you she died?"

Joe nodded his little head as much as he could and still cling to her. "Yes, he told me. He didn't tell my brothers. He told them she was gone on a long trip. Then he said I was old enough to know the truth. He said we couldn't have a funeral but I don't know why. I just want to see her one last time."

"Of course you do, Joe, of course. I'm sorry it's not possible right now." Roxanna had to bite her tongue to keep from blurting out the truth. Not knowing what to say, she asked Joe, "How about I sing you a song to help you sleep?" Without hesitating, she started "Abide with Me" in a sweet soft voice. After the first verse she felt Joe relax in her arms, so she released him and let his head rest on the pillow. By the time she completed the third verse, he was deep into a blessed sleep. She rose and checked the other two little ones just to be sure, but George and Will must have gone down as soon as they landed in their own beds. She braced herself at the top of the stairs to think for a few minutes, then headed down.

"Fran, time to turn in, no back talk," Roxanne snapped. It was clear from her tone that it was not a request. Fran went up the stairs as ordered. "Albert," Roxanna said when Fran had gone upstairs, "we need to have a talk."

TWELVE

A NEW LIFE

LYDIA HAD PACKED ONLY AS MUCH as she could get into the valise Uncle Jesse had given her when they took their trip to Louisville. As she walked the moonlit road, she thought about the girl she had been eleven years and a lifetime ago. Looking back, it seemed her existence was divided into chapters with the titles being life-changing words that had been spoken to her. Hearing her mother tell her brother Jacob, "Your sister has the devil in her," was the first big chapter. It summed up her childhood. "Always remember what you saw here today," spoken by her Uncle Jesse while she watched that young girl being sold in the Louisville slave market, would be the title of the chapter on her social enlightenment. The next would be about her disillusionment when her Ma said, "That fool old man. There is no money for you to go off to school, Lydia." Finally there was, "Albert was wise to tell us you intended to run off with that boy," from her own mother's mouth the day she confronted her about the big lie. That would be the chapter about how she lost her family altogether.

Although she knew the road she walked like the back of her

hand, the way to the spring was rough in the dark of night. It was a relief when she saw the dim light of Duncan's lantern by the crossroads where he had waited patiently since dusk. She shifted her valise from hand to hand as it grew heavy along the way. Suddenly Duncan was there beside her sweeping her up in his arms, the bag slipping from her hand as she threw her arms around him in return. They stood just like that while time stopped for a minute or an eternity, Lydia could not tell which. Duncan broke the spell when he spoke the words that would be the title for the next chapter of her life.

"My love for you is eternal, Lydia. No one could ever fill the spot you left in my heart."

"Nor you in mine, my sweetheart," Lydia replied. "I have only been half alive since that day they told me you were leaving Kentucky. I love you."

When he released her and picked up the valise, a surprised grunt came from his mouth. He laughed and said, "You carried bricks for almost two miles?" He could not see Lydia blush in the dark.

"I'm sorry, Duncan, I brought a few books and all my recent journals. I simply could not leave them behind."

"Of course, my dear. Just wish you had not had to carry that heavy a burden such a long way."

It seemed to Lydia he was talking about more than books. She felt tears pooling in her eyes and falling down her face. She hated that she cried so easily, spilling out her emotions for everyone to see, but here in this moment, in the dark before the dawn, they seemed entirely right.

"We need to go quickly," Duncan said as he reached the buggy and loaded the valise. "It will be daylight soon, and I want us to be far from here when the sun comes up. "

It was an anxious trip for them both. Lydia did not question her feelings for Duncan, but she felt the tug of the little ones she'd left behind. As the sun rose higher in the sky, she tried to imagine what they were doing each hour of the day. Duncan was fearful Albert and his relations were mounting a search party that would end badly for both him and Lydia. Wary of being recognized if they caught the train in Beaver Dam, Duncan paused twice to trade for a fresh horse so they could make it to Owensboro by the evening. He relaxed a bit as they reached a tavern familiar to him near the train station, where they would board a coach to take them to Chicago the next day. After getting Lydia set up in a room and carrying their few things up the steps to the second floor, Duncan took the horse and buggy back to the livery where he had hired it and lingered long enough to settle the bill and give Lydia a few moments alone.

When he returned to the room, he hesitated, then knocked. Lydia opened the door, and holding a covered tray, he stepped into the small well-appointed room they would be sharing for the evening. They both felt immediately awkward as they focused on the central feature of the room, the brass bed adorned with a faded patchwork quilt. "Shall we have dinner?" Duncan asked, setting the tray down on a small table by the bed.

"Do you want to wash up a bit first?" asked Lydia. They both stood without moving for a long moment. Then she added, "I have already had my turn at the basin. I emptied it but I put fresh water in it for you." Duncan took off his jacket and hung it on the chair, moved his suspenders off his shoulders, and started removing his shirt. Lydia blushed and stammered, "Goodness, after all that sitting today perhaps I'll take a short walk before dinner. I will step out and let you have a bit of privacy." Duncan smiled and continued to undress, never letting his eyes leave her face. Lydia found herself rooted to the spot on the floor unable to look away from his body as he removed his shirt. He dipped a clean cloth in the basin and then stretched the wet cloth out to her.

"Perhaps you could stay and help me. I'll walk with you later." Lydia took a step toward him, but when she reached for the cloth, he said, "I don't want you to get your dress wet helping me." Then he began to undo her bodice. She gave not a mummer of protest as he continued until she stood before him in only her chemise. All she could think about other than her sudden wantonness is that he seemed to know a lot more about removing lady's garments than he should.

He finally handed her the wet cloth, and she started the task of bathing him, but it soon was clear that he was not especially interested in cleanliness at the moment. Only when he unbuttoned his trousers and let them slide to the floor did she realize he was still wearing his shoes. He moved to the chair to remove them and then pulled her toward him as he sat. As she stood in front of him, he lifted her chemise and started kissing everywhere his mouth could reach on her naked body. Lydia gasped as he ran his rough fingers and soft lips over her breasts, her waist, her hips. When he stood and lifted her last remaining garment over her head, she put her arms in the air to help him and then moved her fingers to the buttons of his shorts. In seconds they were pressed together skin to skin while his mouth explored her neck, her face, her lips.

Lydia had only been mounted from behind in her years with Albert, something he doubtless copied from the barnyard animals with their same lack of finesse. Duncan leaned back and gently explored all the sensitive spots of her body while asking for her direction on what gave her the most pleasure. She gave in to the new and delicious sensations as her body awakened to the game he taught her.

"Yes, there, there. Oh yes, there." As the tension of her body reached a peak, a shock wave of orgasm washed over her. For the first time in her life she understood the joy men and women could bring to each other. When she felt she could take no more pleasure, she begged him to stop. Instead, he rolled her over and pushed into her. The press of his body against her brought more exquisite contractions. She cried out as she relinquished all control of her body, her very soul. Time stood still as they lay there entwined and exhausted.

Finally Lydia broke the spell. "I never . . . I mean I could not . . ."

"Nor could I," Duncan responded. "You know, I have been with other women, but being with you is better than all the dreams I had for all those years."

"I never even dared dream. You were a boy when I last saw you, and all I knew about sex before tonight I learned from a thoughtless brute." Overcome with emotion Lydia started to sob.

Duncan's heart broke for her and for himself. He held her until her body stopped shaking.

Finally he said, "I cannot erase yesterday, my darling, but I can promise that for the rest of my life I will love and cherish you, the way it should have been from the start. I am not rich, but I am well situated and have good prospects. When we get settled, I want to make those dreams you always had come true. School, travel, anything, and of course at night we will have the wonderment of each other's bodies." With that he started kissing her tears away, and it was clear the comfort would soon lead to passion.

"Sweetheart," Duncan whispered, "before we start again, perhaps we should have some food to keep up our strength?"

Lydia laughed. "So soon after your promises something else is more important than me?"

"Nothing is more important than you, my love, but if you want more delights tonight, I will need a bit of cheese and bread to keep me going."

"By all means then, eat," Lydia said as she fetched the covered tray and propped it in her lap as she sat shamelessly naked in the bed. After they finished off every bit of the summer sausage, cheese, hard bread, and fruit, Duncan was true to his word. When the morning light came through the curtain, they still lay entangled in an exhausted sleep from several repeat performances in the night.

The sun was well risen when they fully woke. "Hope we're not too late for breakfast," Duncan whispered in her tiny ear that was so close to his mouth. He had been reluctant to disturb her although he had been awake for a while, just breathing in the delight of her soft auburn hair and the unblemished white skin of her shoulders.

"If we are, there is always the dining car on the train," Lydia replied. She yawned and stretched. Any shyness she might have felt the night before was gone as she threw off the covers and headed naked to the washbasin. Duncan lay and marveled at the beauty of her form as she washed. Finally she turned to him, scolding him gently. "Lazybones, time to get up. We have a train to catch."

She took his breath away when she turned. His first instinct was to call her back to bed, but reluctantly he realized they had many miles to go before the day was done. He rose and headed to pour fresh water in the wash basin. A half hour later they were both dressed and packed. Breakfast in the dining room was mostly over, but they were able to get a cup of coffee and some rolls to tide them over until noon.

Lydia was over her romantic notion of train travel by the afternoon of the second day of the long tiring trip to Chicago. It did give the two of them time to make plans for how they would manage when they got to her new home. She did not want to have to lie about their status, but neither did she wish to be assumed immoral. They agreed they would keep the lie simple since Lydia was not likely to run into anyone she knew in Chicago. She and Duncan picked a wedding date, April 21, and made up a courtship that was as close to fact as they could keep it. Lydia reluctantly agreed they would not tell anyone about her husband and children. When the afternoon train slowed and entered the outskirts of the city, Lydia's nose was pressed against the window glass. Duncan tried to tell her about what she might see, but nothing could prepare a woman from an isolated Kentucky farm for a bustling city of almost three hundred thousand people.

When they got off the train and out of Union Station, Duncan steered her toward a line of Hanson cabs. He choose one, gave the driver an address, and jumped in beside Lydia for the ride to his sister's house.

Lydia began to feel anxious again. "I just wish I had time to clean up before I see her, Duncan. I've been in this same dress for days."

Duncan could find no fault in her looks. "She'll understand, my dear. Josie will take you right to your room and let you freshen up."

"I'm not sure I can call her, Josie. The last time I saw her she was my teacher. I can't call her Miss Porter, of course, because she's married. Tell me her husband's name again."

"Maxwell Carpenter," replied Duncan, "but everyone calls him Max. Their children are Billy and Anne. You'll be calling them by their first names before the day is out."

Lydia did not feel any more confident. She would have to tell lies to survive. She struggled with how that was different from what her parents did to her, what Albert did. Trying to keep all the untruths straight made her stomach churn.

Her heart was racing when they finally pulled up in front of a large stone house with an ornate front porch. There were trellises with roses that had been trained to grow from the ground up to the roof of the first floor, all abloom in shades of pink. By the time Duncan had helped her down from the cab, her old teacher was standing beaming on the steps. Two shy little faces peeked out from behind her skirts, their eyes big with questions.

"Lydia!" shrieked Josie Carpenter in a most unexpected manner. "I am so excited to see you again! Duncan, take her straight upstairs to the guest room. I'll have Lottie prepare a bath for her. Let me take your things and have them washed. I put out an old dress of mine that I think might do for this evening until yours are all clean." Josie made a grab for Lydia's valise and was startled to see her almost jump back from the encroaching hand.

"Please, Miss Porter. Don't take my bag." Lydia's voice took on a panic-stricken tone as she clutched all of her worldly possessions close to her body.

"You may call me Josie, my dear, and I am so sorry. Your trip here must have been exhausting and the city somewhat daunting."

Lydia felt the heat rising in her face. She had embarrassed herself on the very first step onto her future sister-in-law's porch. "No, no, it is I who should apologize. I must seem ever so ungrateful for your hospitality in welcoming me into your home. I am so sorry. It's just that I brought mostly books and journals. Duncan told me we would buy appropriate clothing once we arrived. I only have one change of costume in the bag."

"I am delighted to have you with us, Lydia. I think my excitement for you and Duncan overpowered my common sense. Please come in. Consider this your home."

Lydia took a deep breath and aimed up the steps for the open door into the most elegant house she had ever seen.

A scant hour later Lydia was transformed by warm water, soap, and clean clothes. She protested when she saw the outfit Josie had laid out for her as it was much nicer than anything she had ever owned. Josie agreed that it was a lovely dress, but unfortunately she had a few stubborn extra pounds she could not seem to shake since the birth of her last baby. Josie laughed and admitted, "Since baby Anne is now five, I think it is time to give up hope." When Lydia came down the stairs that evening for supper in the sheer peach gown with its crisp white underdress, Josie noted the look in Duncan's eyes when he rose to greet her.

Josie said with admiration, "It fits you perfectly, my dear, and the color with your skin and hair is lovely." Josie then turned to the rather plain gentleman who was standing behind her with five-year-old Anne and seven-year-old Billy attached to his legs. "This is Max, my dear. Children, unstick yourselves from your father's legs so he can greet your auntie." The children giggled and reluctantly let go. Maxwell Carpenter stepped up to take Josie's proffered hand.

"Welcome to our home, Lydia. I want you to think of it as your home, too, for as long as you like." Max was rounded and jovial with eyes that twinkled, a smile that was infectious, and a slightly receding hairline. Lydia liked him as soon as he spoke.

Dinner was roast chicken that had been cooked with carrots and tiny new potatoes. The fresh green peas were the best Lydia had ever eaten, just barely steamed in what Josie called "the French fashion." Dessert was a rich eggy caramel pudding with a dollop of cream. When coffee was served, Lydia leaned back and patted her waistline. "Another meal or two like this one and your dress will not fit me! That was simply delicious."

Josie gave all the credit for the meal to her cook. Lydia had seen the young woman who filled her bath and the man who served their food, but did not realize how much household help the Carpenters had. Never having been around many free Negroes, she was curious about their status in Chicago where no one had supposedly owned slaves for over a hundred years. She was very surprised when Josie called the cook out to receive compliments. "Rose," Josie said, "this is Duncan's wife, Lydia. She had something to tell you about the meal."

Rose looked Josie right in the eye when she spoke, something that suddenly struck Lydia because it was not usual in Kentucky. Rose's dress was drab, but her hair was tucked into a brightly colored turban. Her white apron was starched and ironed stiffly, and although she must have taken hours in the kitchen cooking, it was spotless. She had even features and skin the color of the café au lait Lydia had been served long ago in the Louisville hotel where she went with Uncle Jesse. She turned her intelligent amber eyes toward Lydia waiting for her to speak.

"Rose, what a lovely name and what a wonderful meal! I have not traveled far, but I cannot imagine anything in a fancy restaurant being better. The green peas were especially good. How did you make them taste so fresh?" Rose's lips began to turn upward as Lydia spoke.

"I put them on a bed of leaf lettuce with just the moisture that clings to the leaves when they are washed. Then I place them on the coolest part of the stove just until they simmer. The secret is to use very fresh peas and not to cook them too long. Then I add butter and a few leaves of fresh mint." Rose spoke like an educated woman who knew her worth. Lydia was intrigued and determined to get to know this formidable woman better.

"You must show me, Rose. I only know country cooking. It seems like I have a great deal to learn."

Rose smiled and nodded. "I used to work in one of Chicago's best restaurants, but they wouldn't let women do any of the fancy cooking. I learned a lot just watching while I was peeling potatoes and washing dishes."

Lydia longed to follow Rose back to the kitchen and start her lessons right away, but looking around the table at uncomfortable faces made her pause.

"Sounds like an interesting time, Rose. I look forward to hearing more." From the looks she got, it seemed she had said something wrong, so Lydia just gave a puzzled smile and stopped speaking. Silence followed while Rose headed back to the kitchen along with the young black man who was finishing clearing the table. Duncan was the first to speak.

"Thank you so much for the wonderful meal, Josie. You and Max will have to excuse us. Lydia and I are still tired from our long journey, and we have much to do tomorrow."

"Of course, Duncan. We understand completely." Max winked at Duncan as he spoke, not realizing Lydia saw. Of course, the Carpenters believed them newly married, which was as good as true. Goodnights were exchanged as the couple headed to the privacy of the elegant guest room with its draped canopy bed and new mahogany furniture. As happy as Lydia was to finally be alone with Duncan, she resisted his advances until they had a conversation.

"What did I say that upset your family, Duncan?"

He looked at her uncomfortably and pretended not to understand. "You said nothing wrong, my dear. Do you need help getting your dress off?"

"I need the truth, Duncan." Lydia put on her most stubborn face, and Duncan already knew her well enough to realize he could not brush off her concerns.

"It's complicated, my dear, but I'll try to explain. I know you have never been in a home with servants, certainly not in one with Negro freemen as servants. We treat them well and pay them a fair wage, but they are not our friends, my dear. You will be expected to maintain a certain distance. Surely you can understand that."

"No, Duncan, I can't say that I do understand. It is outside of my experience. I recall Uncle Jesse talking about how he and Burwell, the son of the slave his mother freed, was his close friend and companion in childhood. Burwell's mom and dad were their neighbors and friends until they sold their farm and moved north before the war. I suppose I always just thought that's the way it should be. Of course, I have never forgotten the slave auction I saw in Louisville before the war or the stories of how Negroes have been abused. I guess I thought that was just in the south and that it was over now. I can see I have been naïve." Lydia was trying to be reasonable, but she felt her anger rising at what she saw as injustice. Duncan seemed to be stubbornly clinging to a slanted view of what was occurring under his very nose.

"I'm sorry, Lydia. I see you feel very strongly about this, and I know I have not given it enough thought. Can we possibly talk about these things tomorrow when we are both rested?" The day had been long, and they had not had any private time together since the inn where they spent the night in Owensboro. Lydia's eyes softened.

"Of course, darling, and yes, I do need help with my dress." Soon all thoughts of anything other than skin touching skin were banished as the world narrowed to the width and length of a soft feather mattress.

THIRTEEN

CHICAGO, CITY OF CONTRADICTION

LYDIA WOKE to the startling pealing of church bells. She shook Duncan awake to find out what was happening. "Might be a fire, but it's pretty far away. Probably on the other side of the river. Nothing to worry about," Duncan told her.

Being unused to the realities of city life, Lydia insisted on getting dressed and checking. Duncan took her to the window on the stair landing where they could see the tiny plume of smoke in the distance on the south side of the Chicago River. "The fire department will have it out pretty quickly. Let's get breakfast, and then I'm going to take you shopping like I promised."

"But, Duncan, you have taken so much time off from work. Won't they be expecting you?"

Duncan smiled. "I have until next Monday before I have to head back to the office. I'm on my honeymoon, you know, Mrs. Porter."

It took Lydia several seconds to realize who he was talking about. Then she smiled and put her arms around him. "It will be a while before I am accustomed to answering to Mrs. Porter. Shopping does sound wonderful. Can we see some of the city while we're out?"

"Most definitely, my dear," Duncan confirmed as they headed down the elegant stairs. "I must tell you, even though Chicago is a large city, it is a hodgepodge of buildings, some being magnificent, but many quite shabby. I want you to be safe, so I will fill you in on areas to avoid, but if you are ever in doubt and I am not here, just ask Josie or Max for help."

Rose had coffee, fresh baked rolls, thin slices of ham, and several types of jam set out on the sideboard. Lydia was a bit embarrassed that everyone else in the house had already eaten and were on with their day. Little Anne, not yet old enough for school, came in to sit in Duncan's lap and gave Lydia a jealous stare. Suddenly she announced, "I'm going shopping with *my* Uncle Duncan today. He's going to buy me dresses and shoes and a dolly."

Lydia did her best to repress a laugh. Clearly Anne had been told about today's plans and did not want to share her beloved uncle.

"But Anne," Duncan said with great seriousness, "I wanted to buy you a surprise and I cannot do that if you are with me, now can I?"

"What's the surprise?" Anne asked immediately, clearly intrigued.

Duncan burst out laughing and tickled Anne's tummy. "You rascal, you almost tricked me. If I told you, it wouldn't be a surprise, now would it?"

Anne giggled happily and chatted with both adults until breakfast was finished. Lydia listened with joy and kept a smile on her face while a teardrop fell on her plate and then another. Anne noticed before Duncan did, almost before Lydia did, and reacted with dismay.

"Why are you crying, Auntie Lydia?"

Her words melted Lydia's heart but not as much as her jumping down from Duncan's lap and coming to pat her cheek. "It's all right,

Auntie Lydia. You can go with Duncan today. I won't be mad at you."

"Oh, you sweet child," Lydia choked back a sob. "It's not that. It's just that you remind me of another little person that I love and miss so very much."

Duncan was touched when Anne opened her little arms and Lydia pulled her in for a hug.

"I have an idea," he said. "On Sunday we will all go together to the new zoo that has just opened in Lincoln Park. They have a real wolf, Anne, like the one in *Little Red Riding Hood*."

"Oh, oh, oh and bears, do they have bears?"

"Not yet, but I'm sure they will soon. Now scoot off and find your mommy. Be sure and tell her about the wolf."

Anne skipped out of the dining room calling, "Mommy, There's a wolf! Mommy, Wolf!"

Both Lydia and Duncan were still laughing as they rose from the table and prepared to leave.

Duncan held out his arm for Lydia to take as they started down the steps. "Here's our carriage," Duncan said as he pointed to a trap hitched to a handsome dappled grey. "It's the best way to see the city, plus we can talk." Duncan looked a bit serious now.

"What a beautiful animal!" Lydia exclaimed. "I'm excited to see more of Chicago. I do need to get some stationary today so I can start writing to the boys." Lydia paused for a minute and then added with a catch in her voice, "I wonder what Albert fed them for breakfast this morning?"

"I'm sure he's taking good care of them, Lydia," Duncan told her as he helped her into the trap and took the rains from the groom. "Try not to think too much on it for your own sake." "Of course, you're right, sweetheart," Lydia agreed, a bit too quickly.

As they stepped out onto the path in front of the house, she looked around more critically than she had the night she arrived. The rose trellises on the house were grimy with soot from the many coal fires of the businesses that operated throughout the city. The block where the Carpenters lived was in a section of fine homes, but they did not travel far before they came across a jumble of mean unpainted hovels, livery stables, outdoor markets with live animals for sale, hardware stores, dry goods shops, grand churches, and the occasional tavern.

Duncan headed the horse north on LaSalle Street and paused briefly in front of the impressive stone courthouse. He explained that the two-story tower in front was manned around the clock by a sentinel who could communicate with boxes around the city and dispatch firemen to the right spot to put out a blaze quickly. He then headed on toward the river and crossed the bridge on State Street.

"Now I want to show you the other reason why you don't have to worry about fire here in Chicago." When Lydia looked up, she saw the top of a high tower rising more than a hundred feet into the air decorated like a castle from a fairy tale. Duncan continued to explain that the tower contained a large pipe that carried water from two miles out in Lake Michigan into the city where it was used by homes and the fire department. When Lydia started asking questions about how it worked, Duncan told her, "Ask Maxwell tonight. I think I told you he works with a group of engineers in the city. He did not directly work on the water tower, but he will be able to explain it much better than I can."

After circling around the tower, the horse clopped off down Pine Street and back over the river on yet another bridge. Lydia was astounded by how Duncan found his way through this maze of streets, and she was totally lost even though he explained the route as they went along.

"Now we're on State Street," he said. "Time to stop and do some shopping."

Lydia had a look of confidence and excitement on her face as they walked into Palmer's Marble Palace, but her grip on Duncan's arm let him know her self-assuredness was less than a dime deep.

She had never owned a garment that she or her mother did not make with their own hands. Two hours later she and Duncan walked out laden with packages on which her "husband" had spent an exorbitant sum of money. The bulk of their purchases would be delivered later that day: hats, shoes, gloves, yard and yards of fabric for new dresses, not to mention all the undergarments, including two new corsets. The one thing that would take some getting used to here in the city would be having to wear the constraining steel-ribbed underpinnings on a daily basis. Josie had already suggested it was best to unlace it an inch or so at night rather than removing it altogether, "to maintain your tiny waist," as she said. Lydia had held her tongue as she could not point out that after carrying three children her waist was not an inch larger than it had been before the births. She began to suspect that perhaps men had invented these torture devices to restrict women.

Lydia tried to establish some sort of routine in the next few weeks and to find her place in the household. Josie organized several afternoon teas to introduce Lydia to her friends and acquaintances. It soon became apparent that her relationship with Josie was going to be warm but uncomfortable. Having first met as teacher and student, Josie was finding it difficult to find another way of relating to her former prize pupil. The maternal role she felt toward her younger brother was extended to encompass his new wife, making things doubly complicated.

It was most fortunate that Duncan had taken on a new role with his company where he would be in charge of the sales team and no longer travel as extensively as he had in the past. She loved having him home each evening, but her days without him were filled with idleness. Under Josie's instructions the servants took care of the running of the household; the cooking, the cleaning, the laundry, the mending, and the care of the children were already in their capable hands. When Lydia tried to be useful, her efforts were frowned upon. When she arrived in the kitchen one afternoon for what she hoped would be cooking lessons, she was greeted by a sudden silence. She haltingly tried to ask for instructions and was met with blank stares. Finally Rose asked if she would like a cup of tea. Thinking it an invitation for a sit-down chat, Lydia eagerly agreed. Then Rose told her to go relax in the parlor and she would have it to her momentarily.

Josie found her holding the cold cup in her hand a half hour later, tears spilling down her face.

"Oh, Lydia!" Josie exclaimed. "Whatever is wrong? Did one of the servants say something inappropriate to you? I won't have them being disrespectful. Tell me who did this and I will speak to them immediately."

Lydia felt even more distressed at the thought that Josie would punish one of the servants simply on her word. After a lifetime of hard work and unfair treatment, Lydia had found herself forced into inactivity and thrust into life with a class of people beyond her understanding. She could not explain to Josie that she identified more with the help than she did with Josie and her friends.

"Oh no, Josie, everyone has been very courteous toward me. I had hoped to learn more about Rose's cooking by watching, but I guess I approached it the wrong way. I am so unused to idleness. I have my writing, of course, but that does not take up all the hours of my day. I should have asked you before I approached Rose. Perhaps you could talk to her for me?"

Josie frowned. Lydia could see her trying to pick her words carefully. "My dear, I know you are unused to servants. Please try to understand. The darkies are a simple people. They are not like us, and they feel uncomfortable around their superiors."

Lydia felt the heat of anger rising in her face at the pejorative term and the attitude toward an entire group of people. She would have expected this from Southern sympathizers but not from the Yankees who had just fought a war to free them from slavery. She had to speak, but realizing her position, she had to be very careful.

Stealing her emotions, she started, "My dear sister, my experience with Rose is that she is a bright and formidable woman, far my superior in many areas. She can read and write, keeps the household accounts for you, and makes sure all the other staff does their work. In the past months I have been here, it seems to me that you find her indispensable. Of course, as you correctly pointed out, I have no experience with servants. I could certainly be wrong in my reading of her intelligence and drive."

Josie's face grew dark. She was angry at Lydia's correct perception of the situation and frustrated that she was being pushed to acknowledge them. It was undeniably accurate that Rose was exactly how her sister-in-law described her. When she spoke, however, it was clear she had no intention of admitting the obvious truth. "You are right, my dear. You have no experience with servants. Rose works under my guidance, so it is I, not she, who keeps the house running smoothly. I'm sorry but I must ask you not to speak to her directly in the future. It will only confuse her. Are we understood?"

Lydia heard the schoolmarm authority in her voice. She no longer felt cowered by the tone, as she often had to use it on her own children, but she knew there was no future in arguing further with her sister-in-law.

"Yes, Josie, I understand completely." Then she added, "Thank you for hearing me out."

Both Josie and Lydia stood, then embraced. Neither wished to do so, but women learn very early that they must behave civilly regardless of how they feel.

That evening Lydia lay tangled in Duncan's arms and the sheets twisted about them. "That was wonderful, my love," Duncan whispered. "I had to bite my tongue to keep from screaming with pleasure."

"You take me to such heights, sweetheart. I feel exactly the same. I hate having to worry about your family hearing us. I suppose we really have no choice, though." Lydia knew the power of silence. As she waited, she ran her nails gently along Duncan's bare back, causing him to shiver in pleasure.

Finally he spoke, "Well, to be honest, my dear, there is no reason why we have to live with my sister now that I have the new position. It was always convenient before when I traveled and was only home every few months, but now that I'm here every day, we could look for a little place closer to my office. It's just that we could not afford to live in the same style my sister does, at least not for a while. I couldn't ask you to do all the work of running the house alone."

At this Lydia could hold in her relief no longer. Her body shook trying to laugh quietly. "Oh, Duncan," she gasped, "I think I can handle a small place with just you to care for after managing a farm house in the country and three children. When can we move?"

"We'll start looking tomorrow since I have a day off." Duncan kissed her again and ran his hand along her body as she lay naked there in the moonlight.

"One other thing," Lydia said in a teasing voice. "Your sister tells me I should wear my corset to bed in order to keep my figure. I suppose I should start right away."

Now it was Duncan's turn to hold in laughter. "Best you come to our bed wearing only what the good Lord gave you, my sweet little vixen." Lydia started laughing as she drew him close.

"Have I ever told you about the conversation I had with my Uncle Jesse about my namesake great-grandmother? I asked him if his mother was notorious. I was only around eleven or twelve at the time and really didn't understand what the word actually meant. I never imagined I might earn that title someday, but here I am naked, shameless, and eager for my lover's body." Duncan smiled and reached for her again.

Later when they both fell into a deep, peaceful sleep, Lydia dreamed of living in a tiny house on a barge floating in Lake

Michigan, nothing around them but water as far as the eye could see.

JOSIE SAID ALL the right words, but it seemed to Lydia she was not at all disappointed to see them leave her house. She had pitched in enthusiastically to help with furnishing and decorating the small but well-situated house Duncan had found for them with his brother-in-law's help. Never having had the opportunity to pick out what she wanted in her own home, Lydia had to put her foot down firmly many times to keep Josie from overriding her choices. She was careful to remain effusive in her praise of her sister-in-law for taking her shopping to all the best stores and also to little out-of-the way places where bargains could be found. When she was finished, their little oasis in the city was filled with rich jewel tones and touches from faraway places where Lydia had always wanted to travel. A wall hanging from Japan, a Turkish vase, a little French side table were all artfully placed in the comfortable book-lined sitting room. A small dining table fit in the large alcove created by a bay window that looked out over a quiet street. In the back of the house was a serviceable kitchen that led onto a broad covered back porch. The steps to the two small upstairs bedrooms were tucked between the front parlor and the kitchen. The first night she and Duncan spent alone in their tiny dormered bedroom, Lydia found out just how much he had been holding back while living at his sister's house.

The weeks and months that followed were the happiest Lydia and Duncan had ever known. The love that had drawn them together at the start soon grew to a tenderness and adoration so deep Lydia became fearful it was undeserved and might be taken away in the blink of an eye. As the familiarity between them grew, it seemed to increase the passion that always sat just below the surface of their peaceful companionship.

When Duncan was not working, he delighted in taking her to see the sights of the city, as viewing them through her eyes was like seeing them for the first time. When they went to the Chicago Historical Society, she stood with her hand over her heart viewing the original copy of the Emancipation Proclamation in Lincoln's own hand. That evening they had talked about her namesake, the great-grandmother she never met but admired more than any living woman. They talked into the night about her views on slavery, on Lincoln, on the future of the divided States after the war and his death. Lydia spoke for the first time in her life without censoring her opinions.

"It is the great tragedy of our generation and for untold genera-tions in the future that Lincoln was cut down before he had the opportunity to try to reunite this broken country."

Duncan had always respected Lydia's quick mind, but until that night he had still held onto the prevailing opinion of the day that women were not capable of understanding politics. It was very clear to him that he had been wrong. He had watched her as she poured over each newspaper he brought home, and in her impatience to learn more she had even walked to the market and spent her house-hold money on additional publications. Her thirst to know and understand what was going on in the world was astonishing to him considering her upbringing. He had thought to free Lydia from what he saw as bondage. He began to understand that regardless of her circumstances, her stubbornness and her intellect had kept her from giving in to despair. She was unfettered in her soul always and now in her person. He had freed her body, and she had returned the favor by freeing his mind. In truth Lydia's keen intellect humbled him, but it also made him proud of her.

After that evening he became determined to find a way to get Lydia into Northwestern University where he had been a student before the war. He recently heard they were accepting women into classes. He would make some inquiries before he got her hopes up, but he went to sleep very determined to make it happen that evening.

For Lydia's part little effort was required to keep her little house tidy and put meals on the table. She found herself with ample time to keep up her journals and read books borrowed from her brother-in-law. Finally she braved a long newsy letter home to her dear friend and coconspirator, Beth. Before many weeks passed, she got a letter in return which she opened with a mixture of excitement and dread. Beth was straightforward about the reaction around the county over her disappearance. "The wags have been so delighted to spread the news that the pastor preached a sermon on gossip last week," she quipped. Lydia smiled at Beth's attempt to make light of her unforgivable sin. She went on to tell her that Albert had taken in two of the Renfrow girls to help out with the children and they seemed well enough from what she could tell. The news that little George sat snuggled in Roxanne's lap all though church services was both a comfort and a heartbreak. That night she woke with a scream caught in her throat thrashing against Duncan as he tried to wake her from another nightmare.

"Darling, it's okay, I'm here," he said softly and calmly.

Lydia tried to recall the reason for her scream, but it vanished as soon as she was well awake and all she could tell Duncan of her terror was, "There was a red man."

"An Indian?" Duncan queried, puzzled.

"No," she responded in a sleepy voice, "he was *red* red." Duncan surmised she was making no sense.

"It was just a dream, darling." He patted her gently and held her as they both drifted back into a restless sleep.

FOURTEEN

MEPHISTOPHELES

LYDIA WAS MOST grateful when the hot, dusty summer of 1870 began to fade into the relief of autumn. Had it not been for the one large tree in her backyard that shaded the open porch, she would have spent the dog days of August prostrate. As much as coming to Chicago had excited her, she had not been prepared for the crowding, the traffic, the dust, and the stench of so many humans and animals in such close proximity. Added to that had been what the locals said was an unusually dry year. Her little kitchen garden had flourished only because of the many buckets of water she had lifted from the backyard well and poured over each plant. Duncan told her there was no need to grow her own produce because of the abundance in the city markets, but he still seemed to take a certain pride in her skill in encouraging cabbages, carrots, turnips, and potatoes to spring from the tiny backyard and pole beans to climb up strings along the back porch. Now with November upon them and the feel of snow in the air, all of Lydia's bounty was stored in the root cellar beneath the kitchen. She felt a sense of satisfaction as she sat down to write a letter to Beth and one to her boys. Deep in thought, she had not heard Duncan's early arrival until the front door suddenly burst open and there he stood smiling mischievously.

"Oh, my dear one, you startled me!" Lydia exclaimed. "It's not long since noon and I have not started supper. Why are you home so early?" Lydia looked from the twinkle in Duncan's eye to the large box in his hand. "Whatever is in the package?"

"You'll have to open it to find out." Duncan beamed at her and set the box on the dining room table.

"For me?" Lydia was pleased but concerned that Duncan was spending too much on her. "I have everything I need, sweetheart. You shouldn't keep buying me things."

"Not quite everything," Duncan said with a broad smile.

"Let me get this ink off my hands," Lydia replied, then scurried to the kitchen. When she returned, the strings on the enormous box were cut and whatever was inside pushed at the lid. She caught her breath as she opened it and beheld a sea of emerald-green satin. Her amazement grew as she lifted the gown out of the box. It was the most beautiful dress Lydia had ever seen, off the shoulders with a black French lace overlaying the bodice. Under it there was a matching cape and a feathered ornament for her hair. Delighted, but puzzled, Lydia looked up at Duncan and said, "This is spectacular, my dear, but where will I ever wear it?"

"To supper and the opera to celebrate your birthday," Duncan replied with obvious enjoyment at the perplexed look on Lydia's face. "Tonight," he added.

"What? Tonight? My hair . . . How can I possibly . . ."

"Best get started, my love. The carriage picks us up at seven. Oh and one more thing." Duncan went back to the front door and opened it. There stood the young girl who had helped her dress at Josie's house. "You remember Betty, don't you, Lydia?"

"Ma'am," said the timid girl with a slight curtsy.

"Betty is going to help you get ready. Josie and Max will be joining us along with a few of their friends."

Lydia's startlement did not last long. Duncan smiled as she sprang into action.

"Oh Betty! It's so good to see you. Can you help me draw a bath? I'll show you where everything is. I'll need shoes and . . ."

Then Lydia noticed two parcels in Betty's hand. "Here are the shoes, ma'am, and Miss Josie leant you some of her jewelry."

Lydia propelled herself across the small room and into Duncan's arms. "You are the most amazing man I have ever known, Duncan Porter. I could have worn the peach dress Josie gave me. Oh my goodness, the *opera*! I'm going to the opera!" At that point Lydia burst into tears. Duncan could not hold back his laughter.

"Well, don't cry about it, sweetheart. Just go get ready."

Three hours later Lydia was sitting at her dressing table while Betty fixed the feathers and bows to her freshly coiffed hair and then hung the emerald necklace around her neck. Lydia stared at herself in the mirror feeling like a character in one of the fairy tales she had read in her Uncle Jesse's library as a child.

"Miss Lydia," she said, "you look right pretty."

Lydia surprised Betty by taking her hand and pressing it to her cheek. "Betty, you were a godsend. I would still be in my petticoat if you had not come and helped me. I can't thank you enough." Betty blushed and pulled her hand back.

"You're welcome, Miss Lydia." Betty stammered a bit. "And . . . uh . . . thank you for being so nice to me. Some white folks act like I'm a slave they can order around. You treat me like . . . well, almost like a friend." Betty looked surprised that the word had come out of her mouth.

"I don't know what it's like to be born a slave, Betty, but I know all about being treated like less than a person. My family—" Realizing she had almost started to tell Betty about Albert and her parents, she stopped abruptly.

"Anyway," she continued, "I could never treat anyone that way."

Betty's smile seemed genuine, but sometimes it was hard to read the Negroes she met. Lydia could not blame them for being guarded. Still she congratulated herself for making a breakthrough with the young servant girl. Later, when the carriage dropped Betty off at Josie's house, it occurred to her that no matter how intelligent, courageous, beautiful, and gracious Betty might be, her darker complexion and tightly coiled hair precluded her from identifying with the fair-skinned heroines in fairy tales. In a world of injustice the plight of Betty and her kin seemed the most fundamentally inequitable to Lydia.

Thinking of her own situation, she felt a deep wave of guilt. The characters in the fairy tales found their happy ending because of their inherent goodness, luck, and perhaps a bit of magic. Lydia had no illusions about her goodness since she had cheated her way into this dream. She had retreated so far into her head with these dark thoughts that she was oblivious when Josie and Max were climbing into the carriage until Josie's teacher voice jolted her. "Did you hear me, Lydia?"

"I'm sorry, Josie. This all seems like a dream to me. I think I must be afraid I'll wake up." Lydia managed a little laugh to assure Josie. "I should be thanking you for your part in selecting this gown and loaning me jewelry."

Josie beamed. "My pleasure, dear. You look exquisite, like a princess in a fairy tale."

Lydia was stunned at the reference. It was almost like Josie was reading her mind. She shyly shook her head in denial. Josie turned to Duncan and said, "Now doesn't she look just like a princess, brother?"

"More like a queen." Duncan smiled and picked up Lydia's hand. "The queen of my heart." The intimacy of his expression seemed to embarrass everyone in the carriage, but Lydia most of all.

"Max," Lydia said to fill the awkward silence, "tell me about the opera we're going to see." Max beamed as it was a subject he could speak about for hours. The two engaged in happy chatter the rest of the way to the theater.

ONE AREA of Lydia's education that Uncle Jesse had neglected was music. She had only read about opera, but neither the hymn singing at the Baptist church or the fiddle playing at country parties had prepared her for Marie Seebach singing Faust. Although she smiled and clapped along with the thousands of people in the vast auditorium of Crosby's Opera House, she could not follow the story in a foreign tongue. Max provided a whispered narration of the dark, tragic tale that was very disturbing to Lydia.

During the intermission she chose to stand but to stay in their box and take in the décor. The fantastic domed ceiling was still high above them although they had walked up many sets of steps to find their places. It was encircled by paintings of great composers, most of whom she did not recognize. The walls were filled with larger-than-life frescoes, each more elaborate than the next. Then there was a cut stone structure that sat at the front of the stage above the orchestra. As the audience began to return to their seats, Lydia delighted in taking in all the gowns, jewelry, and furs.

She began to feel a bit less like a princess when she saw the extravagance around her. Duncan took her hand in his and whispered in her ear, "Crosby spent six hundred thousand dollars on this building. Wait until you see his restaurant where we're going after the show."

Lydia gasped. It was an impossible amount of money. What did a man have to do to make that much money anyway? No time to ask as the curtains parted again, the devil Mephistopheles returned to the stage, and Max continued to translate the terrifying detail of the script.

The restaurant after was as amazing as Duncan had indicated, but it was all but wasted on Lydia as she had no appetite. Perhaps it was the late hour or the scene of the soprano Marguerite in prison or maybe just her tightly laced corset, but she felt nauseous as she pushed the expensive morsels around her plate. When Duncan caught her eye, she realized she was not doing as good a job of covering up as she thought.

"Darling, are you feeling alright?" Everyone turned toward her after he spoke.

Lydia smiled her best dazzling pretense of happiness. "What could possibly be wrong on such an evening, sweetheart?"

Alerted, Josie put her hand on Lydia's forehead to check for fever. "Duncan, you need to get Lydia home. She is pale and she feels very warm. Max, call for the check."

Max dutifully raised his hand toward the waiter even though Lydia insisted she was perfectly fine. "I will never forgive myself if you cut this wonderful evening short because of me. Please, just order me a cup of hot tea. No need to fuss."

Reluctantly, Max ordered the tea, and Lydia drank it while the rest of the table finished their dinner. She did feel a bit better afterward but was still not herself on the ride home. After Duncan helped her out of all her constricting clothing, she did feel much better, but she was fearful she knew exactly what her ailment might be. Tomorrow would be time enough to talk to him about her concerns. Tonight she just wanted to feel his arms around her, his mouth on hers. The waning moon was still bright enough to cast a glow of silver over the room, the sheets, and their entwined bodies.

She did not wake Duncan with the terrified scream from her nightmare because it trapped itself in her throat, where it dwindled to an anguished squeak when she fully awoke. She lay there exhausted and drenched in sweat although the air in the room was icy cold and grey with the Chicago dawn. She slipped quietly away from Duncan's sleeping body, found her robe, and tiptoed down the narrow stairs to stoke the fire.

The gas lamp did little to help chase away the phantoms in the shadows this morning. She started breakfast, stoking up the fire, putting coffee on to perk, and getting biscuits mixed and ready to put in the oven when it was good and hot. She was just dropping salt pork in the big skillet when she felt a hand on her waist and let out a scream. Duncan spun her around quickly, as startled as she was at the reaction. "Darling, who did you think it was? Is something going on?" He held her close, and she felt the fear and tension drain out of her body. He was a man who knew just to hold a woman when she needed holding.

Once calm, Lydia pulled back and said, "Sit down, sweetheart. Let's have some coffee and talk." She moved the skillet to the cooler side of the stove, popped the bread into the oven, and poured each of them a fresh cup. After a long pause while she looked in vain for the right words, she finally just blurted them out. "I think I might have a baby in me, Duncan. I am not sure, but I missed my monthly and I have been feeling a bit off." Lydia was not sure what his reaction would be since she was not sure how she felt herself. The pain of having left her three boys behind had not eased with time, yet her joy in being with this wonderful man grew deeper each day.

"Oh, my darling girl." Duncan's look and the touch of his hand on hers made it clear he welcomed the news. "I was afraid . . . I mean, I thought you might be upset with me. This is more than I ever dreamed. Are you sure that's all, my love?"

Lydia took a long look at his still-sleepy eyes and imagined for a minute a little girl with that same mop of golden hair. Then her stomach churned again with a nameless dread. "I am afraid, Duncan." He waited in silence for her to name her fear. "In the dream I had this morning, I was running through what seemed like hell. Albert was there along with my parents, my children, and an enormous crowd of people I did not know. The ground was burning and rocky, and I was barefooted and almost naked. Everyone was laughing and throwing rocks at me as I ran. I woke screaming just as I could feel the hot breath of whatever monster was behind me."

Duncan rose and then fell down on his knees in front of her chair taking both her hands in his. "My darling, you must forgive yourself. You made the best choice you could under the circumstances. That damnable opera last night triggered this guilt. I should have known better than to take you. What can I do to make this better?"

"No, love, it's not your fault. You've given me more joy in these last months than I've ever had in my life. It's just the lies, Duncan, all the lies. I feel like I constantly have to be careful not to slip up in front of your family, your friends, even the servants. I almost blurted out something about my children in front of Betty last night."

Lydia's head was bent in shame, but Duncan lifted her chin and said most earnestly, "I have an idea, but first perhaps you might want to get the biscuits out of the oven and the salt pork off the stove."

Lydia jumped up and rescued the breakfast. The bread was a bit browner than normal, but Duncan swore he liked it that way. She even opened one of her precious jars of plum jam that she knew was his favorite. As they ate, Duncan told her his idea. "We will have to keep it very quiet of course, but I have a lawyer friend in Indiana. He could help us contact Albert and get you a quiet divorce. As soon as it is final, we will slip away and get married. That way the baby will be born legitimate. Of course, we still won't tell Josie and Max, but it will be one less lie."

More dark thoughts filled Lydia's mind. "I need to ask, Duncan. Would you have suggested this if I had not gotten pregnant?"

Duncan hesitated for a bit longer than she would have hoped. Finally he said, "Of course, my dear, but I think I need to be entirely honest with you. In the long years when I thought you were lost to me, there were some other women." Lydia's flash of jealousy fled as quickly as it came. She wondered now why he had never elaborated on his earlier affairs, and she realized she had simply not wanted to know the details.

Duncan's head was still slightly down as he told her his story. "I had a few silly dalliances when I first came to Chicago. I thought one was true love but later found she was just using me, and for my part I just confused lust with love. I was determined to be more cautious going forward, and I was for many years. Then when I was in the army stationed in Ohio, I made a good friend named Fredrick. We were both officers and he lived near the camp. One evening he invited me to his home when we were not on high alert, and he and his wife and I had a wonderful evening, lovely meal, brilliant conversation. Then his wife excused herself while Fredrick and I sat and drank cognac in front of the fire.

"I could tell he had something pressing on his mind, so I told him point-blank that if I had done or said something to offend him, to please let me know and we could work it out. He laughed and said no, but he had something to say that he hoped would not offend me. I waited for him to find his words.

"It seemed that an injury when he was young had left him . . . damaged. When he met and married Clara, he found he could perform, but they had been trying for eight years now to have a child with no success. He stuttered around a bit and then asked me if I could give him and his wife what he could not. I admit I was very taken aback, but just at that moment Clara came into the room in a revealing nightdress.

"Fredrick glanced at her and then at me, giving his approval, and then left the room. Clara took my hand and bade me follow her. I had not been with a woman for a number of years, and when she came into my bedroom, I found it impossible to resist her allure. We made love that night and for several nights after. She always left me as soon as we finished, and then we all met for breakfast like nothing had happened. Things went on like this for several months with me visiting, her slipping in and out of my room at night, and then the normal breakfast. We were getting ready to leave for combat the last time I visited, and I found Fredrick increasingly angry at me because Clara was not with child. The troop fought one last battle and then came word that the war was over, Lee had surrendered. We all headed home, and I never heard from either of them again.

"I wondered for a while if Clara might have been the one who could not conceive, but when I came back to Chicago, Josie mentioned casually in conversation about the horrible bout of mumps I had when I first came to Chicago and how she had laughed at me for looking like a squirrel with an apple stuffed in each jaw. "

Lydia sat stunned. "So you think the mumps might have left you sterile?"

"I do not know. I had thought perhaps, but then when you say you think you are expecting, I have to think it is likely I'm not. It's too long for it to be Albert's, so it would have to be me. I have thought of marriage so often, but I know how much you have missed your boys and were hoping to hear something from Albert that would give you hope of perhaps seeing them again. It has been months now with no word except the news from Beth. I was going to bring it up in the spring, but there is really no reason to wait. I will write to him today."

Lydia thought of the last depressing letter she had gotten from Beth. Albert had wasted no time whispering the story of his unfaithful wife and unfit mother to everyone who would listen, which included the entire county. She was grateful it was done in whispers so the children did not hear, but she felt a sharp pain that no one had defended her, not even her brother Josiah. In fact, he and his wife had quit coming to church. By now the gossip had died down, and the congregation seemed to accept Roxanna and Albert sitting in the church pew every Sunday as a couple along with the boys. She was heartbroken to read Beth's statement that "the children seemed to adore their new mother." She knew Beth's intent was to let her know the boys were happy and well treated, but it hurt to think she was so easily replaced. What neither she nor Beth knew was that the boys believed her dead but were forbidden to talk about it to anyone.

Duncan's letter to Albert was sent off the next week, but they received no response until right before Christmas. It was a cold, bitter Chicago day when the news arrived in the form of a spiteful letter from Albert. When Duncan returned home from work that evening, he was alarmed to find Lydia sitting in the darkened room staring into space with the letter in her lap. He busied himself lighting the lamps and stoking up the neglected fire before he sat down beside her and took the letter from her unprotesting hands. After reading it over, he pulled her to him and held her close in his arms. Only then did she start sobbing with the great gulping cries of the heartbroken.

Finally the rage and pain subsided enough for her to speak. "I left all those letters for the boys and have been faithfully writing to them every week, yet all that time they have been mourning their dead mother. They do not even have the comfort of talking about it to their grandparents or their uncles."

Duncan tried to find words of comfort for her. "Albert is not an introspective man. I think your departure took him totally off guard. I imagine he made up the lie quickly, and once it was spoken, he could not retreat from it. One thing I know for sure, my darling, is that the truth seeks always to be free, and in this case there are so many people who know, it will not be chained for long."

Lydia was drained of tears, but the knot of grief in her throat still made speaking difficult. "Would that not even be worse? If they find out years down the road that I am alive and believe I left them without a word, they will hate me."

"We will take precautions to make sure that does not happen, my love. Keep writing your letters to them and mail them to Josiah. He is still close to the boys and will make sure they get them when they start asking questions." Duncan paused briefly while Lydia thought the idea over. Finally he continued. "I have some other news from my lawyer friend that I hope will help. As you know, he did reach out to Albert and he agreed to the divorce. It will be published in the paper of course, but only in Indiana. Locals in Kentucky will not see it nor of course anyone in Illinois. With any luck it will be final long before the baby arrives in May."

Cheered a bit by the thought, Lydia rallied. "Speaking of the baby, I think she is telling me to eat despite my own lack of appetite. I did start that stew earlier today before the letter arrived, and hopefully the stoking of the fire has warmed it up." Duncan declared the thick pork stew with potatoes, carrots, and onions delicious and perfect for the cold evening. The two of them talked late into the night making plans for staying with Josie and Max over Christmas and taking the trip to Indiana in the spring for their secret wedding.

Lydia sealed away the pain of her letter in that dark spot of her brain where she tucked all the other disappointments of her life bound safe for now with the light of her current joy. She woke feeling buoyant and blessed, but rising from her bed, she saw the red stain on the sheet. If there had been a child, it was no more. Perhaps it had all been her imagination, the little girl with the golden curls that matched those resting so peacefully on the pillow beside her. She kissed him gently. The news would wait until her love awakened.

FIFTEEN

ICE AND FIRE

By Christmas time they had both justified the loss of what never was. Lydia was relieved that Duncan still wanted to move forward with the divorce so she could be his legal wife. She was stunned when he told her that he wanted her to apply to be a student at Northwestern University. He had held off telling her his plan when he thought her pregnant, but now the news was welcome and very exciting. At first she protested that she would be the only thirty-year-old in class, but Duncan assured her that would not be the case.

Josie and Max invited them to parties around town with their friends and then for Christmas dinner at their house. Little Anne played happily with the homemade doll Lydia had fashioned for her from fabric scraps she salvaged from a neighborhood dressmaker. Josie complimented her on the cunning little costumes she had made for the plain little rag doll with its embroidery eyes and mouth. An expensive new glass doll with an elegant silk dress sat quietly on the sofa staring at them with a look of disdain. It had been opened first, but it came with a warning to Anne about the care she must take in playing with it. Little Anne assessed the situation quickly and left the fragile treasure in a safe place while she dressed and redressed her rag doll. She was forced to put it aside when she and Billy ate supper, but she carried it off to bed with her while the adults had a grand feast in the festive dining room. On the way home Duncan commented to her about what a wonderful mother she would have been to their baby.

Lydia was glad for the dark so he did not see the tears streaming quietly down her face.

JANUARY of 1871 arrived with a fierce snowstorm that turned the previously muddy streets to a pristine white and decorated the porch with deadly-looking icicles as the sun warmed the roof. Lydia enjoyed the first day of the storm, but when it snowed again the next day and the next, she began to think she was in for a long winter. Getting out of the house to purchase food was increasingly difficult because of the condition of the streets, which were partially frozen waves of mud, ice, and horse apples. In late February Duncan started going with her to the market on Saturday for fresh meat and whatever staples were running low. She was grateful for the fur-lined cape with matching bonnet and muff he had given her at Christmas, as the wind and cold turned her face raw and red. She held tightly to Duncan's arm and inquired, "How much longer can winter possibly last?"

"Oh, another month at the most, I think, maybe two." Duncan responded with no hint of irony. *Well*, thought Lydia, *another thing about Chicago I was not prepared to face*. By the time they reached home with their purchases, her eyelashes were frosted with crystals and almost frozen shut. She stoked up the fire and put the pot on for tea to take the chill off, then put away her purchases while Duncan cleaned snow off the front porch again and brought in more wood. By the time the tea was brewed, she had set out a cozy lunch for them: her homemade dark bread, cheese from the market, and sliced apples from her winter storage under the kitchen floor. Warmed and nourished Lydia tidied up the little house and anticipated a rare afternoon of relaxation and writing while Duncan puttered around in the barn.

She had no more than sat down before Duncan came through the back door and announced, "Get on your warmest things. We're going for a sleigh ride." As cozy as she had become, when Lydia saw the excitement in Duncan's eyes, she set her journal aside and quickly tucked herself back into the clothing she had hung near the fire to dry only an hour before. Outside the horse was stomping and blowing steam in his eagerness to exercise. Duncan tucked the warm rabbit fur throw over them and snapped the reins. "Gee up, Merry!" he cried, and off they flew.

The wind was chilling as they rushed along, even colder near the lake, but the weather did not deter any of the other young couples who shouted greetings as they passed on the busy streets. Judging by their age, Lydia soon realized that most of them were sparking singles. It delighted her since she and Duncan had never had the opportunity to be a carefree young couple. She snuggled closer and tried not to think about all the years they had missed. She marveled at the transformative power of the cold and snow. The streets that were a mire of mud and animal waste in the fall were magical trails of pristine white. Crisp clean air replaced the fetid autumn stench produced by masses of people and animals. Even the meanest hovel took on a picturesque quality when softened around the edges by snow, and the mansions with their turrets and ginger-bread gables became fairytale castles.

"Someday," Duncan proclaimed, "Chicago will be a grander city than St. Louis or even New York. We will look back and say we remember it when it was a gangling adolescent still rough around the edges."

In that moment Lydia could see Duncan's vision: a great city on the shore of an inland sea, trains carrying goods and people to and fro, a center of arts and culture, and the two of them perhaps living in one of the fine houses along Michigan Avenue filled with books and intellectual friends. Lydia slipped the memory of this crystalline moment into her heart to treasure later when summer's heat had turned it all to slush and mud again.

She thought of that magical moment often in the next months as winter melted into spring and spring into a desperately dry summer. After the last rain in early July the heat soon turned the mud to dust, which whirled around the city in choking clouds, leaving every surface covered. For the rest of July and all through August and September so little rain fell that keeping her tiny backyard garden watered was half of all she accomplished during the day, and often the rest seemed to be taken up with battling the omnipresent dust.

When Duncan arrived home in the evening, she had to resist the urge to voice complaints about things that were not in anyone's control. That included her divorce, since the last time they talked about its progress, she had resolved not to bring it up again unless Duncan did. After his initial agreement Albert stubbornly resisted signing any papers to complete the process. The application she had filled out for Northwestern was unsent as she could not complete it until she was free from Albert and married to Duncan. Lydia continued to write letters to the boys although trying to keep a tone of desperation out of the one-way conversation was difficult.

She knew Duncan grew restless at times in his new position. Although it paid well, he had grown accustomed to escaping the confines of the city in the heat of the summer. Now the tedium of endless paperwork and discussions in an office with the unrelenting heat, buzzing flies, and cloudless sky ate at his soul. But her heart still skipped when she heard his step on the porch in the evening, and the look of relief on his face as he gathered her into his arms told her he felt the same. Their little dormered bedroom was sticky hot long into the evening, but it did not keep them from reaching hungrily to each other every night and often again as the morning light came slipping through the gauzy curtains.

One early morning as they finished, Duncan spoke, "I always knew you were my touchstone, but I could not have imagined the passion we'd share. We are twin souls, my love, and I want to secure your future. As soon as the weather breaks, I am traveling to Kentucky and demanding Albert sign those papers. If anything should happen to me, I have investments I intend for you to have so you can finish school."

Lydia shushed him. "Please don't talk about anything happening. I cannot bear the thought. There would be no life for me without you." Duncan pulled her near again to reassure her, but the seed of concern he planted fell on the fertile soil of Lydia's imagination.

LATE SEPTEMBER CAME and still the sky refused their pleading and prayers for rain. Added to the constantly blowing hot wind from the south was the smoke from forest fires that raged in Minnesota, Wisconsin, and Michigan and prairie fires that smoldered near the city. During the first week of October hardly an hour went by without the courthouse bell sounding out a fire alarm somewhere in the city.

When the bell started ringing that Sunday night, neither Lydia nor Duncan paid it any attention. Hours later Lydia woke with a start and realized that the bell was still pealing. She slipped on her robe and went to her window. The entire southern horizon glowed red. Startled, Lydia went straightway to rouse Duncan. "Wake up, darling. I think the fire is near us, Duncan." She pointed to the bright red landscape outside their window. He looked briefly and then started pulling on his clothes.

"I'll go outside and take a look. Get dressed just in case, sweetheart. We can go to Josie's."

Lydia was dressed and had her valise packed when he returned. "I hitched up the carriage. We need to go now. It seems to be headed this way." Lydia took one last look around her cozy home. She had little more in her valise than when she had arrived in Chicago, a change of clothes and her journals, but as long as she had Duncan, everything else could be replaced.

The smell of smoke and the unnatural hour made it difficult to control the nervous horse. Lydia was glad for Duncan's sure hand on the reigns as she looked back over her shoulder at the blaze. "I can't be positive, but it seems it has crossed the South Branch of the river."

Duncan's gaze at the road ahead did not alter. "Yes, that's what the man I saw outside said. He was headed to the lake. He said the wind is blowing it along and it seems unstoppable. We need to get Josie, Max, and the children up and out of their house too."

As they headed toward Michigan Avenue, they were surprised to see groups of people going toward the fire laughing and obviously drunk. "Fools," quipped Duncan. The deafening roar of an explosion sounded, and gas lights flicked and extinguished, leaving only a blizzard of sparks and ash to light their way through the darkened streets.

The Maxwell Carpenter household had been roused by the explosion, and Max was in the process of waking the servants and getting his family ready to flee when Duncan pounded on the door. Max had already sent the servants to hitch up his calmest mare to the largest carriage, then directed them to take the rest of the animals and go rescue their own families. By the time everyone was tucked into the carriage, the fire was almost upon them. Anne was clutching her rag doll and sobbing about leaving some remnant of the doll's costume behind. Billy's face was a mask of fear striving for bravery. Josie rung her hands and fretted at leaving her beautiful house with only her jewelry and one change of clothes for each of the children.

Max, grim and resolved, tried to quiet her. "The house is insured, plus it is made of stone. The city is well prepared for fire with the pumping station to keep the water running. Besides, we have our most precious items right here," he said, glancing at the anxious children sitting between them.

The frightened horses would hold no longer. Duncan gave Merry the signal, and they rushed forward followed closely by Max's carriage. They had not gone a mile before the chaos of the city overwhelmed them. Everywhere the streets were filled with fleeing people, some with carriages but most on foot. Uncertain of the extent of the fire, the masses headed in every direction, some east toward the lake, some north to the river, some inexplicably west or south toward the obvious wall of fire. The streets were littered with items hastily thrown out of windows, mattresses, quilts, trunks, artwork, birdcages, furniture, and piles of loose clothing being trampled in the mud.

Duncan and Max climbed down and began unhitching the panicked horses, both of whom bolted as soon as they were released. There was nothing to do but to abandon the carriages, pick up the children and follow the mass of people trying to find refuge from the blaze. Josie quickly tucked all of her jewelry into pockets as Lydia tied her small valise to her back with the sash from her dress. Max and Duncan scooped up the children, and they headed grimly for what safety they might be able to find.

In order for fire to die, there needs to be water and, usually, lots of it. In the desperate hours of Monday morning October 8, 1871, the water works that pumped lifesaving liquid from the boundless inland sea of Lake Michigan was hit by a burning timber thrown out of a whirling firestorm. In minutes the machinery was gutted and useless. With no water to fight the blaze it spread effortlessly from building to building. Despite gallant efforts by firefighters and citizens with buckets, about one third of the existing city was destroyed before it started to rain the morning of Tuesday, October 9. The death toll was estimated at around three hundred souls, but because of the intense heat of the fire it is believed that many others fell uncounted, totally consumed by a blaze that razed block after block.

SIXTEEN

A WAKING NIGHTMARE

LYDIA WOKE to the unfamiliar sound of rain falling on the makeshift shelter Max had fashioned with half-burned timbers fished out of the lake. Long seconds passed before she remembered the last minutes of Duncan's life and recommenced the hoarse, wailing sob she had begun last night. Josie quickly clapped a hand over her mouth and hissed at her not to wake the children. Silenced, she sunk back into the living nightmare with no hope of waking to find Duncan's reassuring arms about her.

The picture looped over and over in her brain. They were almost across the bridge, pressed on every side by bleary, shocked, and exhausted people. The wave of energy that had propelled them out of their homes had by now drained their bodily resources and reduced their minds and bodies to numbness. Duncan had handed little Anne over to Lydia and took the lead, using his strong body to push them through the crowded escape route across the north river.

The fire had already jumped across the river further west, fueled by grease and debris and destroying all but this last escape. They were almost to the other side when an enormous burning ember fell on a man walking immediately in front of Duncan. Those around him tried ineffectually to back away as his clothing and hair started blazing. In his panic he pushed to the nearby edge of the bridge instinctively trying to jump into the water below to douse the flames. Duncan, seeing the state of the water, knew he would be leaping to his death and attempted to hold him and beat out the fire. His terror seemed to give him superhuman strength as he and Duncan struggled at the railing. As they fought, the man turned his face toward Lydia. When she saw him, she froze in horror. It was the red man from her nightmare months ago, his hair and beard blazing and his face distorted.

The rest of the scene played out in a few eternal seconds. The man gained purchase on the edge and lunged his body over while still flailing wildly at Duncan. With her beloved's arms around the red man's legs, the weakened railing gave way, sending them both into the boiling cauldron of the river below. The throng of people pushed them onward, but Lydia fought her way to the rail a bit further along and peered over. Seeing no sign of Duncan, she unconsciously shifted the sleeping babe to her hip and leaned forward. Josie gasped, thinking that Lydia was trying to follow Duncan. She pulled Anne from her arms with the ferocity of a raging bear and slapped Lydia sharply across the face. Little Anne woke to hear her mother screaming, "Follow him if you want but not with my child in your arms!"

Pushed by the throng behind her, Lydia continued across the bridge like an automaton, more dead than alive. She did not speak a word, but after they found a spot in Lincoln Park to sit, she started making a dreadful keening sound punctuated by great racking sobs. Max came and pulled her under the shelter and begged her to be quiet. As soon as she stopped crying, she fell instantly asleep. Now she had awoken to find her nightmare real and herself being pelted by an ironic icy rain.

For the next few days she had no will of her own. She drank or ate when someone gave her food or water. She moved when told to move and slept when told to lie down. They walked for miles through smoldering ruins to a shelter Max had found for them in an unfamiliar part of the city. On Sunday, a week after the fire, Max woke her gently and put a tin cup of hot coffee in her hands. While she drank it, he spoke to her, "Lydia, you have been talking in your sleep every night. Perhaps it's just bad dreams or absent babbling, but Josie and I need to ask you some questions." A bit of the gray fog lifted in Lydia's mind as she came to consciousness. Josie was nowhere in sight, but Lydia realized what he meant was that Josie had questions and he was sent to ask them. "First I need to know the truth. Were you and Duncan actually married?"

"No, Max." Lydia had no will to lie any longer. "We were trying to get a divorce from my husband in Kentucky. He kept refusing to sign the papers. Duncan is . . ." Lydia started sobbing again, but Max sat patiently. "Duncan was going to go to Kentucky as soon as the heat wave broke and make him sign so we could marry. I am sorry we lied to you." She started to continue on explaining, but Max put up his hand to stop her.

"The other question I have is, do you have children in Kentucky?"

Lydia hesitated briefly. "Yes, Max, but let me explain. You see . . ."

Max stopped her again. "Josie and I feel your place is with your children and your husband. I will figure out a way to get you a ticket home as soon as possible. Neither of us wish to speak of this further."

And that was that. Everything she thought she had slipped away like fairy dreams. The only thing she had left were her journals tucked into the old valise, which she had tied to her back when they abandoned the carriage Monday morning. Like her dress, it was sooty and filled with holes from falling embers, but when she looked inside, her journals were still intact.

Somewhere inside she found a tiny spark of resilience buried deep under her sorrow. Looking about, she saw a line of women waiting beside a hastily drawn sign saying, "Women's Bath House." She went there to stand and wait her turn. Although the change of clothing in her valise was a bit the worse for wear, it was cleaner than what she had on.

She emerged some hours later with clean hair and skin and the fresher dress. Volunteers had taken the dress she had on and washed it while she bathed. She found it hanging still wet on a long clothes line in the yard of the hall where they had rested for the night. With no plan or direction she sat down on a grassy bank and waited for her dress to dry. She barely looked up when she heard her name. "Miss Lydia? Is that you?" Slowly raising her head, Lydia saw a familiar light-brown face etched with concern. It was Rose, the cook who had been so standoffish toward Lydia when she was staying with Josie and Max.

"Where is Mr. Porter?" Rose asked, looking around.

Lydia did not know she had any more tears left, but they started rolling down her cheeks again as she shook her head. Having been turned away by the only family she had in Chicago, Lydia expected no sympathy from a woman who had been decidedly cool toward her in the past. She was stunned but thankful when Rose sat down beside her and put a comforting arm around her shoulders.

"There, there, Miss Lydia. Cry it out," Rose said. They sat there together clinging to each other for a good quarter of an hour. Finally Rose said, "He was as good a white man as I have ever known, and he loved you with all his heart. Few of us ever have that kind of love in our lives. You know, he came to me a few months back and apologized for treating me condescendingly. He said he had just not realized how it must have appeared until a conversation with you opened his eyes."

Lydia stopped sobbing as she leaned back to look at Rose. "I remember when I talked to him, but I did not realize he took it so to heart and then came to you to make it right. He was a truly good man, and I did not deserve him, Rose. I have been wicked and selfish. God has punished me by taking away the only man I will ever love."

At that Rose spoke forcefully to her. "I don't know your sin, Miss Lydia, but I believe in a God of redemption. You have never been anything but good to me or anyone I know."

Lydia spent the next hour pouring out her soul to Rose, telling her all the things the Carpenter family would not let her say. Rose listened patiently, encouraging and asking questions occasionally. When the story was all done, she looked Lydia directly in the eye.

"I hear nothing to convince me that God has any reason to be angry with you. You need to forgive yourself." Lydia was stuck by the fact that Duncan had often used those exact words with her so many times. Then Rose added, "So what do you want to do now, Miss Lydia?"

Lydia shook her head, "I don't know, Rose. I just don't know. I have nothing left. Duncan told me he had some investments that he wanted me to have, but I doubt that any record of them survived the fire. Max and Josie's house is gone, and besides, they hate me now. Max told me I should go back to my husband in Kentucky, which is impossible, but my children. I want to see my children, Rose."

"I will find a way to help you, Miss Lydia. Do you have people there besides your husband?"

"I have one brother who still loves me and a friend who might try to help, but I can't leave like this, Rose."

Rose paused trying to think of what to do. Finally she said, "Come home with me, Miss Lydia. We'll figure something out."

"Oh, Rose, I can't ask that of you."

"You didn't, Miss Lydia. I am offering."

Lydia found Rose's house bursting at the seams with recently homeless people of every race and creed. Rose made sure they were fed and clothed, and tended to their illnesses with her old-fashioned remedies. Most of the locals and all the folks staying with her called her Mother Rose and treated her with great deference. After observing the seeming miracles she was able to perform by conjuring enough food, clothing, beds and love to support them all, Lydia soon discovered the name "Mother" felt most comfortable on her tongue.

Rose put her to work immediately, and after a week of pitching in and helping others, Lydia gradually returned to the land of the living. She became especially close to Rose's orphaned nephew who was around the age of her youngest back home. He was in need of nursing as he had a dreadful cold and cough, even spitting up blood at times. Rose was concerned and wanted to call a regular doctor, but there was no money to do so; plus, there were so many others in worse shape around the city. Lydia was sure the cough was from all the smoke the little one had breathed in the night of the fire. Most everyone who had gone through the worst of it had some kind of cough, including herself. She slept in the rocking chair four nights with him in her lap, his little body hot with fever.

Finally one morning he announced that he was hungry. After he ate some of Rose's nourishing soups, he ran off to play. Lydia laughed as she saw him join in a game with three other children. The resilience of youth was truly amazing, and she felt much relieved that he had recovered.

It was Monday a week after Duncan had perished when Lydia finally opened up her journal again. When she started to write, she found it was still too painful to put the words down. Instead, she started writing about Teddy, Rose's little nephew, telling all the precious things he had said to her. It was then she knew that the only thing that might be able to ease the pain in her heart was to see her boys again. She needed advice and went seeking the person she had come to love and trust.

"Mother Rose," she started. "I think it's time for me to head back to Kentucky. Max told me he would pay the fare for me to go, but I have no idea where he is."

"Are you sure, Lydia? You could stay here. Chicago is already starting to rebuild. There will be opportunities for those willing to work. You have such a fine hand with a needle. Everyone will be needing new clothes now, and I know a lady who would hire you."

"Knowing what I have to deal with in Kentucky, it is tempting, but I need to face up to what I have done." Lydia hesitated a few seconds too long and then added with a catch in her voice, "I don't think I could stand the memories, Mother Rose. Chicago will always be the place where I found true happiness, but without Duncan it can never be the same. That and little Teddy . . ." Lydia choked up again.

"I understand, Lydia. You miss your children. I can contact Mr. Carpenter. I did not tell you, but he sent word to me a few days ago. He wanted to make sure I would be available to work for him again after he rebuilds his house. He sent me a month's wages and said he would do so again in November. His bank burned, but all the records and money were found in the safe still intact."

Lydia was stunned. She assumed everything was gone. Duncan kept their money in the same bank. Perhaps Max would give her enough to get home safely and maybe a few dollars to live on. "Can we find out today, Mother Rose?"

"Yes indeed. We have Mr. Carpenter's horses in our barn. He asked me about them. Let's go saddle up and go talk to him."

The trip through the burned-out city was dismal. There were a few single walls standing here and there amid block upon block of rubble. Gray smoke still hung in the air, and the acrid smell of the air was unrelenting. Crosby's Opera House, which had been recently remodeled and was set to open, was now a pile of charred bricks. The memory of sitting in that magnificent auditorium with Duncan by her side washed over her. It was gone, all of it, the churches, the hotels, the shops; every place she had been with her love in those brief happy days was in ruins.

Illogical as it might be, Lydia felt that somehow the fire was her fault. That perhaps if she had not come to Chicago, Duncan would still be alive and the city intact. She asked Rose if they could ride by the little house where she and Duncan had been so happy. Rose reluctantly complied, but when they arrived in the general area, it was difficult to find a landmark to pinpoint the location. Nothing made of wood remained, not a tree, not a board or well cover. There were only a few columns of bricks from chimneys scattered hodgepodge down the street. Lydia walked to the intersection and stepped off the familiar distance from the corner to her house. She turned where she thought it was and started poking around in the ash until she found the hole that had once been her larder under the kitchen floor. Nothing was left of course; even the metal jar lids were melted. She started sobbing again as she looked around her.

"Oh, Rose, why, why? I should never have written to him, should never have left Kentucky and come to Chicago."

Rose took Lydia by both arms and looked her in the eye. "This fire is not your fault, Lydia. God did not burn down an entire city to punish you."

After Rose said the words, Lydia realized that is exactly what she had been thinking, and at the same time she knew how arrogant it was to imagine she had that much control over anything.

"Thank you, Rose. I have no idea how I would have made it through this week without you. We cannot know God's plan in all this, but I do know he sent you to help me."

"Lydia, the Bible says that the rain falls on the just and the unjust. Sometimes the rain helps, sometimes it hurts, but as far as I can tell, the rain just don't care. I have not seen any miracles in my lifetime, but I do know what people call good luck happens more often to those who work hard to be ready for opportunities." Rose

waited briefly and then added, "Now pick yourself up and let's find
Mr. Carpenter."

THE CARPENTERS HAD FOUND LODGING with a friend from their
social circle until they could rebuild. Lydia and Rose arrived at the
home riding two of his horses. Rose went around to the back door
and knocked. The cook sized them up and told them to wait. After
an inordinately long time Max came out alone with a parcel in his
hand. He spoke briefly to Rose and then handed the package to
Lydia.

"Here are some traveling clothes and money enough to get you
back to Kentucky if you are frugal. Josie and I are doing this only
because of the affection Duncan had for you. Under the circumstances I think we are being very generous."

"Thank you, Max. I appreciate it. If there is money left from
Duncan's investments, can you use it for the children's education? I
know Duncan would have wanted that." It was clear from the
alarmed look on Max's face that there was indeed money left and he
had no idea Lydia had known about it.

Max replied uneasily, "Of course, Lydia, even though you have
no say over Duncan's money. Still, if we find there is any left, it
will go to Anne and Billy."

Lydia smiled. "I understand I have no right to ask, but I appreciate that you and Josie will use it for the children."

Rose stood stiffly listening between the lines of the conversation. Like most of his social class it did not occur to Max that a
colored woman would hear or follow the meaning of what was
being said. He turned to Rose.

"You may take two of the horses to get you home. We will get
them all sorted soon as we get the new house completed and you
come back to work."

"Yessir, Mr. Carpenter," Rose replied, then turned and winked at Lydia. Once out of earshot Rose said, "We'll see about that job later. I have some ideas about starting a business of my own, a restaurant."

Lydia smiled and said, "What a wonderful idea, Rose, and what an opportune time!"

SEVENTEEN

THE ROAD HOME

FINALLY ALONE, Lydia counted the coins still left in her purse. The fifty dollars Max had given her seemed like a fortune back in Chicago, but she was not accustomed to handling money. It had dwindled down much faster than she thought possible. With only eleven silver dollars and a few smaller coins left, she was afraid to spend any on another night in a hotel. Perhaps it was foolish to sit in the cold Nortonville, Kentucky, depot waiting for the early morning train, but with the sky growing pink in the east, she knew it would not be much longer. After today's train ride she would have to have money to hire a horse and carriage to take her to Josiah's or, if he would not take her in, to her friend Beth's house. She was hungry and yearned for a cup of hot coffee, but no one had shown up selling food and she had been warned of the nearby restaurant by an older lady who had shared a car with her the day before.

The cough she carried with her from Chicago seemed to be growing worse sitting in the drafty station. She was glad for the warm outfit Max had given her and felt some sense of comfort in realizing Josie had to have gone to some effort to pick it out for her. It was a serviceable charcoal-gray suit, not new but nicely made of a sturdy wool twill. She had included a black bonnet and shoes that fit well enough if she wore thick stockings and a heavy wool shawl that had been invaluable on the journey. Restless, she had written in her journal until the lead in her pencil became so short it would no longer make a mark. She had all but memorized the dog-eared outdated copy of the *Courier Journal* that a former traveler had left in the station. Exhausted, she dozed off from time to time but always woke with a start, fearful of being accosted by some stranger who might walk into the open door of the drafty little depot.

When a stranger finally arrived, it was a welcome relief—a young woman, shabbily dressed but carrying a basket and a large pot smelling of coffee. She smiled in Lydia's direction and said simply, "Hungry, miss?"

"Oh, my dear, you are heaven-sent," gushed Lydia. "Do I smell coffee?"

The girl set a tin cup on the nearby counter and poured still-steaming liquid into it. "I have no milk or sugar, but I made a batch of biscuits."

Lydia gratefully paid the girl the few pennies she asked, then sat back on the bench to drink the bitter, hot liquid and enjoy her first food since lunch yesterday. When she finished, she handed the tin cup back to the girl who wiped it out with what looked to be a clean but stained dish towel and hung it back with the few others she had attached to her belt.

"Should get busy here real soon, miss. The train is usually right on time as this is one of the first stops." As if on cue an older gentleman with an abundance of bushy gray facial hair opened the front door and headed to the office.

"That coffee still hot, Lula?" he called to the young woman with the basket as he fiddled with a ring of keys. By the time he opened the door and the cage window, she was there pouring him a cup, which still steamed in the cold morning air. He drank it as he set up for the day, opening drawers and checking his watch against the tables. Finally he looked up and spoke to Lydia.

"You need a ticket, miss?"

"I believe I have one already," Lydia answered, "but I would appreciate you looking it over for me." She walked to the window and handed him the packet she had held onto since Chicago. The last one was marked through to Beaver Dam. The station clerk scrutinized it and then looked up at Lydia sympathetically.

"Were you there during the fire, miss? I hear a lot of people were burned out and many died."

Lydia's face lost composure briefly, though long enough for the observant old clerk to see her pain. "I'm so sorry, my dear. Folks around here sent what little they had to help when they heard. You have people in Ohio County?"

"My brother," Lydia choked out, beginning to cry again for the first time in many days. With the tears her coughing started again. The clerk apologized, and the girl, Lula, standing nearby urged her to sit again. She nodded and moved back to the hard bench and sat working to regain the delicate balance she had woven over her grief these past weeks. The coughing fit at least disguised the tears, and the new people who were now arriving at the station avoided sitting near her.

The train thundered in right on time, just as Lula had said. Lydia had composed herself before she climbed aboard for the last leg of the train journey. She began to imagine the faces of her children she had not seen now for over two years. She was hopeful Joe and George would at least recognize her. From what Beth had told her about Will cuddling with Roxanne in church, she doubted he would recall her at all.

The train trip took a bit more than an hour with the stops along the way. By the time she talked the livery stable owner in Beaver Dam into renting an inferior horse to a woman for an outrageous sum, it was long past noon when she pulled up in front of Josiah and Mary's house. The biscuit from her breakfast had only been supplemented by well water since she left Nortonville at 6:09 that morning. A little girl of no more than five years old sat on the front porch holding what she at first thought was a doll but soon realized was a real baby a few months old. "Hello, Becky," Lydia said to the child who was eyeing her suspiciously. "Is your daddy at home?"

"Who are you? Why do you want my daddy?" Becky continued to glare at her. As Lydia drew closer, she saw another little one about two sitting on the porch floor playing soldiers with a box of clothes pins. About that time Becky yelled, "Mommy!!!" at the top of her lungs, causing the startled two-year-old to jump and run to the door and the sleeping baby to commence screeching. Mary burst out of the door ready to do battle, but when she saw Lydia, she stopped stock-still.

"Becky," she said, "give me the baby and go get your daddy from the barn." The two-year-old was hiding behind his mother's skirt at this point, and as Mary took the baby, Becky streaked by her like the devil was close behind her. "Hello, Lydia, I never expected to see you again in this life. Why are you here?"

It was not the warmest of welcomes from someone who had been like a sister to her. Before she could answer, she had turned to face the sound of a familiar footfall behind her. Suddenly she was scooped up into the warm welcoming arms of her little brother.

"Lydia," Josiah said in a shaky voice, "we thought you dead in the fire. Thank God you are okay. Did you bring Duncan with you?" Josiah looked around and spotted the scruffy nag pulling the now empty rig that had brought her.

"No, Josiah," she said with a half sob. "He's not here. I'll explain it all later. I am so very tired. Do you think I could stay with you for a few days until I figure out what to do?" She looked up at Mary, Becky, and the toddler standing in a unified front blocking the front door. The baby was still screaming furiously.

"Of course, Lydia. You can stay as long as you need. We don't have a lot of space with all the babies now, but there is a large padded bench by the fire where you can sleep. Mary, do you have any food left from dinner? You look so thin, Lydia. You must be hungry."

Mary and Becky moved reluctantly into the house, clearing the doorway, but Mary did not try to disguise the look of disgust she gave Josiah. As they got inside, Josiah took the baby from Mary, told Lydia to sit in the rocker, and then put the unhappy little one into Lydia's arms. Josiah seemed to be the only one in the house oblivious to the tension in the air. Focusing on the bundle in her arms, Lydia shifted him to a secure position and began to rock, stroking his soft little forehead with her finger. He quickly stopped crying and fell into a relaxed sleep. Josiah beamed at her and pointed to the little cradle that sat nearby. Lydia put him gently down and then asked, "What's his name, Josiah?"

"Jesse," he said with a gentle smile.

"Oh my." Lydia could find no other words. "Oh my."

"I was thinking of you when we named him, and knowing how much you loved Great-uncle Jesse, I wanted to honor him."

Mary was having none of this sweet exchange. "There is some leftover stew on the table. Becky, take your sister upstairs for a nap. Stay with her until she falls asleep."

Becky took one last suspicious look at Lydia, then did what her mother told her. Lydia was already at the table eating the warm stew and a piece of cornbread. "This is delicious, Mary." Lydia looked up gratefully at her sister-in-law as she finished the last bite. Josiah came to the table, put his arm around her shoulders, and then sat down in the chair beside Mary. They waited in anticipation.

"Duncan died in the fire. We were with his sister, her husband, and their two children trying to run from the blaze. We were on the last intact bridge, and a man in front of us was hit by a flying piece of burning wood. He was trying to jump over the side, and Duncan was holding him back. Then the railing gave way, and the man took Duncan over the side when he fell."

"Did he drown then?" Josiah asked gently, trying to figure out why a jump into the river was fatal.

"No," Lydia said, trying to keep her voice from breaking. "The river was on fire from all the grease and floating timbers. They burned to death almost immediately. I don't think he suffered for long."

Mary sat quietly, and finally she said, "What about his family? Did they die too?"

"No," Lydia explained. "Their beautiful home was lost, but they all survived with just the clothes on their backs and some jewelry. Mr. Carpenter had a lot of funds in the safe of the bank, and they found the safe a few days after the fire with everything inside it secure, including the insurance papers. They will rebuild."

"Why did you not stay in Chicago with them?" Mary asked, sounding annoyed.

"Mary, it is not like you to be uncharitable," Josiah said. Turning to Lydia, he said, "This is your home, sister. Of course you would come here."

"No, Josiah, Mary has a right to ask. I am done with lies forever. They did not want me there when they found out that Duncan and I were not actually married. Duncan was talking to a lawyer in Indiana about a divorce, but Albert refused to sign the papers. Duncan was going to come to Kentucky and talk to him as soon as the horrible heat wave broke. I think he could have persuaded him, but we'll never know now. The Carpenters were angry that we had lied to them. I had begged Duncan to tell them the truth from the start, but they assumed it was my idea to deceive them. Duncan was not there to defend me, so that was that."

"But you walked out on your husband and your children!" Lydia had never seen Mary angry before.

Josiah came immediately to her defense. "You do not know the reasons, Mary, because I have kept quiet. Lydia did not leave without justification." They heard Becky's footsteps on the stairs, clearly trying to sneak down quietly. "We'll discuss it later, Mary. Meanwhile, I need to pick up Abraham at school. Lydia, come with me and bring that nag. We will take it back to the livery owner, and I'll give him a piece of my mind for charging you good money for that old swayback relic."

ABRAHAM REMEMBERED Lydia fondly and was excited to see her when they finally arrived at school. He was full of questions that his father told him would wait until later, and though Lydia had insisted no more lies, she honored her brother's request. While Abraham was almost eight, he was not ready for the all too brutal truth. Her own boys, however, were a different thing entirely. She needed desperately to see them and try to explain. After a night's sleep she could tell that Josiah had spoken to Mary, as the tension around the house had decreased noticeably. Lydia helped Mary with chores in the morning, but when the children settled for the afternoon, she asked Josiah if she could borrow a horse and ride over to Beth's farm.

She found her friend out in her kitchen garden plot putting the last of it in order for the coming winter. Beth ran to embrace her and then pulled her into the house for coffee and a good long chat. Even though they had been apart two years, with Beth it was like starting again midsentence from their last conversation. First Lydia had to tell about Duncan's death, and her dear friend cried along with her. With each new tear a bit of her grief flowed out a little more, and soon she found that Beth had persuaded her to talk about the great joy of the life she had shared with Duncan. Finally Beth told her, "You have really truly lived these past two years. When you speak of Duncan, you are the girl I knew in school. I thought she was lost in those years you were with Albert. I am so happy you had the life you deserved, even if only for a little while."

The conversation finally turned to her children. Beth tried to find a way to soften what she had to say, but it's not an easy thing to tell a mother that her children are fine without her. "Albert let most people know that you left him for another man. Quite the poor-me speech he worked up about it, too, but he asked them to keep quiet about it 'for the children's sake.' Better to think you dead than a fallen woman, he said. Roxanne told me that's what they all believe now. She was not happy with him lying to the boys. I will say that Albert could have done worse than picking her to mind them. She is outspoken, but under it all she has a kind heart. Plus, she is hard-headed as they come and she speaks her mind to Albert."

Lydia tried to absorb all the information. She was churning with raw emotions but grateful to Beth for being honest. Finally she spoke as one who had learned hard truths. "I should probably leave it be, but they are still my children. Lies have a way of hurting more the longer they stay buried."

"I doubt that Albert is going to let you see them, but you could ride over there now. They will soon be out of school and maybe you can catch a glimpse of Joe and George on the road home. It would be best not to speak to them yet, Lydia."

Lydia hugged her dear friend and thanked her for all she had done. Then she took her leave and headed down that familiar solitary road where memories lay waiting behind every tree and rock.

EIGHTEEN

HIS SISTER'S KEEPER

THE BRILLIANT COLORS of fall were mostly gone from the leaves, and the horse picked its way through the rustle of brown that covered the road. At the top of the hill she paused and looked down over the snug homestead where she came as a bride only twelve years ago, before the war, before the children, before Duncan found her, before she lost him forever. She sat on the back of the mare consumed by what-ifs when she heard young voices and feet shuffling through the leaves. She pulled the horse off the path behind some cedar trees where she could watch unnoticed as they passed. George was wearing the shirt she remembered making for Joe, now passed down to his younger brother. Joe's new-looking coveralls were rolled up at the bottoms, and the white shirt he wore under was clearly sized to allow for growth.

Lydia sat stock-still listening to her heart beat in her chest as she watched them pass. It took all of her strength not to call out and run to embrace them. She watched their retreating backs for several minutes before the horse, startled by a falling acorn or maybe the squirrel that dropped it, reared slightly and whinnied. Joe, protector of his younger brother, turned immediately and made eye contact with her for seconds before she was able to gallop away.

Racing back to Josiah's farm, she tried to convince herself that Joe could not have recognized her, although she had seen that spark of awareness and shock in his eyes. By the time she reached the house, she was bone weary. Perhaps all the travel and the events of the past weeks had finally caught up with her, but she wanted no more than a soft place to fall and sleep. Mary looked at her in anticipation, perhaps hoping for help with the children while she got supper on the table. Lydia went directly to her alcove bed in the kitchen and sat down shivering. Gathering up the blanket around her, she went immediately to sleep despite the noise of the children, Josiah's arrival, and the family eating the evening meal.

Lydia felt a hand on her head sometime during the night, but when she opened her eyes, she was not sure if she saw someone retreating up the stairs or if it was a dream. She woke with dawn coming in through the window and the noise of Mary bringing the fire back to life. She sat up and attempted to rise and help, but the room started spinning. Despite the coolness of the morning she felt flushed. When she tried to speak, she started another coughing fit, one of many she had been having over the past week or so. She finally got a few words out to Mary. "I'll get up and help in just a minute, Mary. Sorry for being so lazy. I think I might have caught a cold on my trip."

Mary paused and walked over to her. "It may be more than a cold, Lydia. You told us you have been coughing for weeks, and I believe you have a fever." Putting a maternal hand on Lydia's forehead, she told her, "Stay there and rest. I'll get you something hot to drink." Mary's sudden concern alarmed Lydia. She took stock of her own physical condition for the first time since before she watched Duncan fall off the bridge in Chicago. She had grown used to the pain in her chest, believing it to be caused by smoke damage from the fire. She dismissed the racking cough that disturbed her sleep in the same way. As she sipped the hot coffee Mary had brought her, she realized that the symptoms that should be getting better were actually worse each day. She felt another cough coming on and set her coffee down to prevent it from spilling, grabbing the handkerchief she kept in her pocket. When she pulled it away from her mouth, there was a bright red spot on the white cloth. Startled, she quickly wadded it up and stuffed it back in her apron, planning to wash it later in private.

When Josiah came in from the barn for breakfast, Lydia sat quietly watching the family eat. Mary tried to get her to take a few bites of something, but Lydia had no appetite. She again took to her little alcove bed, and amid all the hubbub of the morning routine Lydia fell back into a deep sleep. Her nightmares had not diminished much over the past weeks, but they had become so familiar by now they seemed, if not friends, tolerated acquaintances.

She woke with the familiar red man staring at her and talking earnestly. Without opening her eyes, she gradually realized that the conversation she heard was not the red man, only Josiah and Mary.

"I understand, Josiah. She is your sister, and I now realize life was not fair for her. It's just that if she has consumption—"

Josiah interjected sharply, "Mary, we do not know what she has or if it could affect the children. We need to get Lydia to a doctor. I will take her into town today."

Lydia pretended to sleep when Josiah came over to wake her gently. He asked her if she would like to ride with him into Beaver Dam, not mentioning the doctor. The last thing she wanted to do was ride over the rough roads in an open wagon on a cold day, but she gave her brother a thin smile. "Well, if you are going anyway, I will certainly come along." She tried to hide the effort required to rise from her bed, wash, and tidy her hair. There was no denying that the dress Josie had loaned her was much looser now, and she barely recognized the pale but flushed visage she saw in the little mirror by the door. As she stood there collecting her shawl and bonnet, she heard Josiah speaking to someone outside. When he opened the door, an attractive young woman with thick black hair and light brown eyes was standing there beside him.

"Lydia," announced Josiah, "this is Roxanne Renfrow. You may remember her from school. She was one of the younger students. She says she needs to speak with you most urgently."

Lydia acknowledged her with a nod, but did not extend her hand. "I do remember you, Roxanna, and your older sister, Rachel. I trust she is well as are your other sisters. Forgive me if I have forgotten all their names. Mary, you don't mind if Roxanne sits for a moment, do you?"

"Oh, goodness no, Roxanne. Where are my manners? Let me take your coat and hat. I think there may be some coffee yet. Can I get you a cup?"

Roxanne shook her head, clearly agitated. "Oh, no thank you, ma'am. I can't stay. I just need to have a few words with Lydia, alone."

No one moved an inch. There was no place in the house for a private conversation except the parlor, which was closed and unheated. Lydia spoke first, "Anything you need to say can be spoken in front of my family, Roxanne. I have no secrets from them."

Roxanne stammered a bit trying to find softer words than she would have used with Lydia alone. "Well, what I came to say is . . . I mean . . . You must not come by Albert's house again, not ever. The boys have finally come to terms with your desertion, and we don't want them upset again." Her piece said, she started to turn to leave.

Then Lydia spoke. "So it's 'we' now, is it, Roxanne?"

Her face turned red, and she struggled again for the words. "No, no, of course not. How dare you think . . . Albert has been a perfect gentleman, and my sister stays at the house with us. Just because you have no morals does not mean no one else does!"

"Roxanne!" Josiah spoke with a barely controlled anger. "How dare you come into my house and speak that way to my sister! You have no idea about her morals. If I told you . . ."

Before he could speak further, Lydia put her hand on her brother's arm and said forcefully, "No, Josiah."

Then turning to Roxanne, Lydia said, "You have said what you came to say. Tell Albert if he has anything else to express to me, he should be man enough to come in person. Josiah, can you see Roxanne out?"

Her brother shut the door none too gently as she exited. When he turned, Lydia collapsed in the chair shaking. "Can I have some water, Mary?" she asked quietly. Mary raced to dip her a cup from the bucket and helped her hold it as she drank. When she finished, she started coughing again in earnest. Josiah and Mary exchanged a grim look.

"Come on, Lydia," Josiah said, scrapping his plans to take Lydia to town that afternoon. "Time to rest. Tomorrow we will go to Beaver Dam and see the doctor."

Lydia fell into an exhausted sleep right away, but she spent a restless night with the coughing waking her every hour. When Mary came down to start breakfast, she found her sitting in the rocker with the rosy glow of dawn giving her color not found in her too-pale face. Josiah came soon after to start on the day's chores. Lydia's voice when she spoke to them was hoarse but determined. "Seeing the doctor today would be a waste of time and money. He will be no better than the preacher would be in condemning me because of what I've done and where I've been."

"Surely there is some medicine he would give to help the cough and ease your pain." Mary had softened her feelings about Lydia over the past several days. The visit of the Renfrow girl had solidified her support. She did not know Roxanne, but she had certainly had a few run-ins with her sisters, who were known in the area for bluntly speaking their own versions of the truth.

Lydia frowned and shook her head. "I have seen the results of 'doctoring' both here and in Chicago. The old quacks have no solutions other than purge, bleed, or dope. They always find a way to blame sickness on the sick and treat them with disdain. The good woman I knew in Chicago taught me some of the old ways and I remember a few things. If you could help me collect wild medicine, we can do as well as any doctor. I recall you having butterfly weed blooming in the summer. If you can remember where it was, dig me a few roots. Josiah, I know you can find a few redbud and dogwood trees and will get me some bark from them. We will make some tea and I will be better."

IN THE WEEKS THAT FOLLOWED, Lydia did improve. Perhaps it was the warming teas that helped her sleep or the encouragement she felt from her family. They had no further word from Roxanne or Albert, but Beth came for a visit with news of the rumors going around. It seemed that Lydia's oldest had recognized her and was asking a lot of questions about his mother returning from the dead. Josiah and Mary were shocked to learn for the first time that Albert had chosen to tell Joe his mother was dead. Lydia's biggest grief was that her son had never read the letter she had left him or any of the ones she had written since. Lydia begged Josiah to take her to church so she could just see the boys, but he put his foot down firmly. Beth and Mary both agreed with him that it would be a mistake and might result in making life harder for the children.

It certainly came as a surprise when the preacher showed up at Josiah's home on a cold, clear day in mid-November. It didn't take long for Lydia to determine who had sent him. Her mother had been conspicuously absent since she had returned to Kentucky, but as was her way, she had been working behind the scenes to manipulate her daughter.

He got right to the point, "I've come to get you to repent the evil you've done to your husband and pray for your soul, Lydia. You have put yourself and your long-suffering husband in danger of hellfire!"

"Since he put me in hell for so many years, it only seems fitting that I return the favor." Lydia had no patience with the man who came in her mother's name pretending to speak for God Almighty. Mary and Josiah looked surprised by her bluntness, and the minister's face turned a bright red.

"You would mock God at such a time! Your mother told me of your arrogance and stubborn pride, but it is worse than I imagined."

"Ask my mother about Uncle Jesse's will, Pastor. Then tell me about arrogance."

The indigent minister was nonplussed. "I know all about your disobedience toward your parents, Lydia. Jesse was a bad influence on you, and your mother greatly regrets allowing you to spend time with him. She is trying to make amends by sending me to give you a last chance to repent. You need to get down on your knees to your parents, to your husband, and to God, and beg forgiveness lest you end up spending eternity in hell with your uncle."

With that Josiah lost his patience. While he was never as close to Jesse as Lydia, he had always had a fondness for the old gentleman who taught him how to play cat's cradle with string, a game he had passed on to his children to their great delight. "That's enough, Reverend. I do not profess to know near what you do about the Bible, but if a good man like our Uncle Jesse is in hell, there is no hope for the rest of us sinners." As Josiah spoke, he rose and picked the preacher's hat off the table and handed it to him. The reverend harrumphed as he put it on his head and went out the door.

After he left, Josiah announced, "I'm going over to see Ma and then Albert. I should have done so weeks ago." The women just stared at him as he rushed out the door.

"I suppose one of us should have tried to stop him," Mary said with a slight smile.

"I'm sure you're right, Mary," Lydia replied slowly, despite the fact that Josiah had not had time to saddle his horse and go. "Too late now." They both smiled at each other, and then Mary rose to get the day's chores started.

NINETEEN

REUNION

JOSIAH WAS TACITURN when he returned home late that evening. Seeing the look on his face, Lydia dared not question him. Neither he nor Mary said anything the next day or the next, and although curiosity was burning within her, she decided it best to let it go. Come Sunday the family headed off to church, with Lydia staying home as always. Later that week Beth came for a visit, and the three ladies got into a conversation about the service. It seems that neither the pastor, Albert, Roxanne, nor Lydia's parents would meet Josiah's eye. When he and Mary spoke to them, they ducked their heads and muttered a muffled greeting. Josiah acted as if nothing were amiss. They could not puzzle out what Josiah could have possibly said to them to cause the reaction. The only thing she knew for certain was the tiny bit of conversation Beth overheard between Josiah's son Abe and Joe, Lydia's oldest.

The two boys, like all the rest of the children, were ready to bolt after their long sentence of sitting without wiggling on hard wooden benches. The youngsters broke free to race outside after the last Amen. Beth had needed to make a trip to the outhouse most urgently and had slipped out with them. It was on the front step she heard Joe ask, "Is my ma alive, Abe? Is she staying at your house?" Beth slowed enough to see Abe nod yes but then moved off the porch when Roxanne burst from the door and pulled Joe away with her.

"If he knows, then I should go to church with you next week!" Lydia exclaimed.

Neither Beth nor Mary thought that was a good idea, but Lydia insisted she should speak to Josiah about attending. Later that evening she cornered him and presented her case. Josiah pondered for long minutes and finally spoke.

"I told Albert that if he sent his paramour back to our home again, that is exactly what would happen."

"Josiah! You called her that and threatened them that I would attend church?" Lydia burst out laughing at the absurdity of the warning.

A slow smile slipped across Josiah's face. "Sure did. Roxanne blustered and flapped a bit about that remark, but after I threatened to start the rumor mill going about their living arrangements, Albert shushed her. From their reaction I would say it is possible that the relationship between them is not quite as innocent as they profess."

"What of my parents and the minister? What did you tell them?"

"Oh, I was worried that might be a bit tricky, but fortunately the minister was already at their house when I arrived. I started talking about Jesse, the will, and the lies that were told. Then I mentioned that I wondered how they would feel if it were widely known that they cheated their own child out of money. I took the case directly to the pastor when I spoke. Ma and Pa were trying to stop me the entire time, which just made it very clear they were guilty. The reverend is not such a bad man after all. He soon realized he had been duped by a one-sided story. Then I threw in the part about Albert and Roxanne's unorthodox relationship and him telling the children you were dead. The reverend couldn't get out of there fast enough. I'm pretty sure he went to visit Albert later."

"My dear brother, I would never have thought you capable of this kind of daring. You have the nerves of a riverboat gambler!"

"Well, my dear sister," Josiah said, smiling broadly, "let's just call it payback for all the times you took the heat for me when I was a child. You were more a mother to me than Ma ever was."

"You are so precious to me, Josiah. I think you have more than paid back any debt you might have imagined you owed me." Lydia paused briefly and then looked at him with such sad eyes, "but this means no visit to church and no seeing my children, right?"

"I fear that is not going to be possible right now. Perhaps in a few years when things have died down. I believe Albert is ready to sign the divorce papers now at least. If I am reading things correctly, he wants to make things legal with Roxanne. Now that I have called them out, he is fearful others will start questioning their relationship. If it is any comfort, I do believe there is genuine affection between them and she has been a decent mother for the boys. They seem to like her."

Lydia choked up at that comment. Her confidence in her ability to mother her own children had been compromised by the strain of her relationship with Albert. She loved the boys dearly, but love is not always enough. Perhaps the best thing for them would be for her to move on, maybe even away from this area entirely. She was sure she could get a teaching job somewhere no one knew her, maybe head west to St. Louis or even beyond. After giving the idea life in her head, she found the great weight of her sorrow and loss overbalanced what would have thrilled her ten years ago. She began to question each decision, each step she had taken. Had she been too impulsive, too inflexible, too unforgiving? Had she made decisions or simply reacted to the actions of others? Was she a player or a pawn in someone else's game?

∽

She slept fitfully that night and for many nights after. Her cough returned with a vengeance, so she was forced to sleep propped up in bed in a sitting position. The only thing she had strength to do all through December was sew and write in her journals. She gave Josiah and Mary part of her remaining money for yard goods and made everyone in the family some item of clothing, often working by the light of the coal oil lamp into the night.

The first snow, along with bitter cold, came right after Christmas. The pain in her chest increased with each cough, and she often woke in the night drenched in sweat. Christmas came and went with little merriment but with much warm family time. Everyone was grateful for the neat clothing she had made them, especially little Becky whose favorite rag doll now had an outfit to match her own new dress.

Most of the month of January Lydia was in and out of reality, like one long fever dream filled with all the terrors of past years along with some happy scenes of her time with Duncan, Uncle Jesse, and her children. Unfortunately, the old devil Mephistopheles always seemed to turn up and spoil every idyllic memory even if he did nothing but sit and stare at her. She came to awareness from time to time, mostly in the dark of night, and often either Josiah or Mary was sitting nearby, sometimes awake and watching but mostly dozing. If she woke during the day, it was because Mary was bathing her or getting her to use the chamber pot or most often trying to get her to eat or drink some of the soothing medicinal tea. Rarely was she able to take more than a tiny bit of what was offered. She woke to full awareness one gray morning with little Becky sitting nearby just staring. As soon as she saw Lydia's eyes open, she yelled, "Maaaa!" while still looking right at Lydia.

Mary looked in her direction and soon came over with a cup in her hand. "Will you try to eat some of the broth I have made for you, Lydia?"

She was surprised to find Lydia lucid, alert, and questioning.

"How long have I been sleeping, Mary?" Lydia's voice was a hoarse whisper. She tried to drink from the cup when Mary held up her head and pressed it to her lips.

"Off and on about two months, I suppose, maybe a bit longer. It's the middle of February."

Lydia was shocked at the length of time she had been oblivious to her surroundings. She found the taste of the broth rallied her and made her aware her body required sustenance. "So long," she said. "I guess that is why I feel so weak and hungry." She immediately realized what a burden she must have been to her only real family. "Oh, Mary, I know you and Josiah have been taking care of me. I am so sorry to have put you through so much. I had thought to leave again before this spell of sickness. I should have stayed in Chicago and found my way after the fire. As soon as I'm on my feet again, I will be out of your hair. I still have a few coins left to get me started somewhere else if I am frugal."

Mary gave her a kind smile and reassured her she was no trouble. Knowing better than to take this assurance at face value, Lydia attempted to rise and start helping out with chores again. She was startled to find she could not lift herself off the bed. "Perhaps a bit of food before you try to get up?" Mary's tone was as if she was talking to someone who was feeble of mind as well as body.

"Yes," Lydia replied, realizing she might not be the best judge of her own powers right now.

"That would be wonderful. Thank you, Mary."

While she waited on the food, Lydia took stock of her body, aware of pain but staring it down mindfully as if it belonged to someone else at some other time. Her hands and arms were nearly incapable of movement. They seemed to be made of some insubstantial matter that shifted like water and could not grasp so much as a spoon. She had not tried using her legs because she found she could not even slide them off the bed. Mary arrived with a bowl of something that smelled delicious and made her mouth water. It was a simple dish of warm milk made thick with toasted bread and sweetened with a bit of honey. Lydia ate it greedily for several minutes as Mary spooned it bit by bit into her mouth, but soon repented when her stomach started cramping.

Mary stopped at once when she saw the look on Lydia's face. "That's enough for now," Mary said as she took the bowl away. "Why don't I brush your hair? I fear we have neglected it these past months." Lydia's long auburn hair had always been a feature others complimented, so despite her guilt at keeping Mary from her work, she agreed.

When Josiah came in a bit later, Lydia was still awake and alert. He was heartened by being able to talk to her but was glad Lydia could not rise and see herself. For weeks now he had watched his once vibrant and beautiful sister fade away until he had started checking her breathing anytime her eyes were closed. Mary had done her best, helping Lydia wash her body and put on a clean white nightdress. She had brushed her matted hair until it lay softly around her shoulders. But her weight had dropped alarmingly, and her skin was so pale as to be translucent, giving her face and arms a bluish cast. Still, after the night sweats and racking cough of the past weeks, Josiah was heartened that perhaps the illness had finally run its course and they could look forward to a steady improvement.

After supper the family gathered around Lydia's little sleeping alcove and read out loud from one of the children's favorite books, *The King of the Golden River*. Mary served everyone warm milk with honey, hoping to get a bit more nourishment into her sister-in-law. The children had grown fond of Lydia and she of them, especially Becky. She came to give her aunt a good-night kiss and asked one of her innocent but soul-searching questions about the story.

"Aunt Lydia, do you think that if the two bad brothers in the book felt really truly sorry for the way they acted, the king might forgive them?"

"That's a hard question, Becky. What do you think?"

Becky wrinkled up her face pensively. "I would forgive them, Aunt Lydia. As long as they said they were very, very sorry to everyone they were mean to—their brother Gluck and the old man and the boy and the puppy—and promised they would never act that way again."

Lydia looked lovingly at her kindhearted niece. "Becky, remember when I first came here and we took that walk down by the stream?" Becky nodded. "We found some rocks that were so smooth we liked the way they felt, and we picked them up and took them with us. Do you still have those rocks, Becky?"

"Yes! Do you want me to get them?"

Lydia laughed as she knew Becky was looking for a way to avoid bedtime. "No, sweetheart, but I want you to remember that once, long, long ago, those rocks were rough like the ones high up on the banks of the big river. After years of being tossed about by the water, they have changed. Perhaps the brothers are like those rocks and the river smoothed them out over time."

Becky looked thoughtful. "So when the brothers got all smoothed out by the river, I bet the king forgave them and made them people again."

"I hope you're right, sweetheart. I hope you're right. Now off to bed with you, moppet!"

When Becky and the rest were all gone, Lydia felt a great weariness come over her. She forced herself to stay awake long enough to write a letter to Josiah and Mary, one to her mother and father, then one to Albert. Leaving them on the table beside her bed, she drifted off quickly. Sometime in the night she heard a light step across the floor and felt someone settle gently down beside her on the bed. When she opened her eyes, Duncan was there in the flesh beside her smiling his sweet gentle smile. He took her hand and said, "Time to go, dearest." She started to protest that she was too weak, but suddenly realized she had more than enough energy to join him on an adventure. Rising easily, she put her feet down into what seemed to be soft green grass, warm from the summer sun.

"Where are we going, love?" Lydia asked, even though she was prepared to follow him anywhere. He pointed to a wooden door in a stone wall that seemed familiar, but she couldn't quite place it. Suddenly the door swung open and light poured in invitingly. Uncle Jesse stood with his hand on the latch beckoning her to come. Behind him she could see a line of happy people smiling and waving at her. One was a beautiful fierce-looking woman with auburn hair exactly the shade of her own.

"Do I have time to say good-bye to Josiah and Mary and the children?"

"No need, darling," Duncan said, pointing to the letters lying on the table. "You already did."

"Of course, my darling, you are right. There is nothing keeping me here." She smiled as she took Duncan's hand and walked with him into the golden world beyond the wall.

EPILOGUE

THE ORPHAN JOSEPH LEE McGEE, age twenty-five, rifled through his late father Albert's papers looking for anything that might help him find the whereabouts of his mother. Finally, tucked under the false bottom of a drawer, he found the letters. The first was printed using small words a child could understand.

To my darling Joseph,

I know this is going to be hard for you but Mama has to leave for a while. Your daddy and I both love you so very much, but I am unhappy with him for things that are hard to explain right now. I promise I will come back and see you as soon as I can and my heart will be sad every day when I am gone. I know you will be a good boy and mind your daddy and look out for your brothers like you always do. You have done nothing wrong, my sweet Joseph. When you look up at night at the moon and the stars that we both enjoy watching, know that I am looking up at the same sky and thinking of you.

Love you always,

Mommy

The big strong man that Joseph Lee had become wept like the eight-year-old whose mother had vanished overnight. He had held in those tears for so long. When his father told him she was dead but not to tell anyone, he had only cried once in Roxanna's arms. A few years later he had seen a specter in the woods that looked exactly like he remembered his mother. He was frightened and perplexed when he ran home to talk to his stepmother, the woman who did her best to take his mother's place.

Roxanna listened attentively but did not offer any suggestions or explanations. That night he went to bed confused and unsettled, but the next morning his father tried to tell him and his brothers that what he saw was surely a ghost. Roxanne gave his dad a stern look, and Albert hung his head like a man caught in a lie. Roxanna then attempted to explain gently to the boys that his mother was living, but since she had deserted her children, she was no longer allowed to see them. When he protested, his father made it very clear that this was not a matter for discussion and they would not speak of her again.

Joe had searched the woods every day for many years trying to spot her again, but she never came back. When his father told him he was going to marry Roxanne, he found the courage to question if it was okay to have two wives. His father then told him that his mother was now dead and buried, but having once been lied to, he did not trust his father's words. There was no opening for further discussion, so Joe had let the wound of her loss scab over unhealed. Always in his heart the lesion festered and spread its poison silently over his days. Now as the tears flowed out, they let some of that toxicity drain.

Roxanne had done her best for them, but worn out from bearing four of his father's children in eight years, she died shortly after delivering stillborn twins, before the doctor could arrive. Joe still remembered his last look at her lying peacefully in the pine box with two tiny twin girls tucked into her arms. Her oldest son, Alva, was only six, his brother Wayne, five. Her two little girls, Flo and Vickie, just four and three. Joe stood at the graveside holding little Vickie while his father cradled Flo. His brothers, George and Will, tried to comfort Alva and Wayne to no avail.

Now his father lay up on the hill above the farm sleeping with neither wife beside him. Roxanne's family claimed her right to rest in the churchyard where her mother and father could tend her grave, and Albert's dying request was to be laid to rest on the hill overlooking the farm beside his son George who had died the year before. Joe and his brothers provided as much love and support to their little half siblings as they could, all remembering what it was like to be left motherless. Now only six years later they were all orphans trying to be both mother and father to each other.

Joe spent the rest of the afternoon reading over all the letters from his mother describing her life in Chicago, always telling him that soon she would come to visit them. The dates on the mostly unopened letters were further and further apart and finally stopped altogether. Uncle Josiah had quit visiting around the same time his mother left, but she mentioned him so often in the letters, Joe determined he might be able to help him find her now that Pa was dead. When he arrived at the Ross farm, it was clear that Josiah had been waiting and hoping for him to come. His uncle embraced him and then said, "I am so glad you're here. I have some things for you that your mother left."

Joe felt a surge of hope, "Do you know where she went? Do you know how I can find her?"

"I am so sorry, Joe," Josiah replied with great sorrow. "Your mother passed away long ago. I buried her quietly in the little grove down by the creek. I can take you there if you want, but first I want to give you all the letters and journals she left in my keeping."

Joe's heart sank again. He did not think his uncle would lie to him, not now. Inside the house Josiah rummaged through a large trunk and pulled out an old valise full of journals and letters. He laid them out in order on the table and told Joe to start at the beginning and read to the end. He knew it would take many weeks, but he offered to let Joe come every day and read so Josiah could answer any questions he had along the way. Winter was almost upon them and farm chores less arduous, so Joe agreed to visit every afternoon until he finished the task.

Winter lingered that year with rain, sleet, and snow continuing to fall at intervals that made planting impossible. Joe came as often as he could and read up on his mother's life from her teen years up until her death. He came to know her as a person, a woman capable of great strength and courage born into a world not ready for her ideals or ambition. He grew angry at times with his grandparents, his father, and with her, but ultimately he forgave them all as she did in her final letters. Josiah told him his father had refused to take the last one she had sent to him or to give any of them to him or his siblings. He hated that George died still thinking his mother deserted him. At least Will would now know the truth.

It was a mild spring day in April when Joe and Will finally visited the spot where their mother's bones lay. There was only a small limestone rock marking the grave, with no name or dates. Had Josiah not led them there, it would have never been noticed. Joe read a few pieces from his mother's journals, one a quote she had copied from Margaret Fuller's book:

> "All around us lies what we neither understand nor use. Our capacities, our instincts for this our present sphere are but half developed. Let us confine ourselves to that till the lesson be learned; let us be completely natural; before we trouble ourselves with the supernatural. I never see any of these things but I long to get away and lie under a green tree and let the wind blow on me. There is marvel and charm enough in that for me."

Will brought flowers he remembered his mother planting around the house so long ago and replanted them by the stone. The flowers still grow there and bloom every spring and summer, but there is no one now living who knows or visits the spot. It matters not, however, as her soul has no purchase in this patch of earth. It is enough that her children survived and had children of their own, some of them daughters and granddaughters who went on to achieve great things like Lydia dreamed of doing and many she never imagined possible. From her sprang doctors and university professors and businesswomen and mothers who reared their children, both male and female, to be fair and honest and to look upon the heart of a person rather than their appearance.

ABOUT THE AUTHOR

Elaine was born in the small town of Beaver Dam, Kentucky, an area of lush green rolling farmland contrasted with the tortured landscape left behind by strip mines. She earned her BS in business and a post baccalaureate degree in Information Systems from Virginia Commonwealth University in Richmond, Virginia. She works as a coach, mentor and quality evaluator for the customer service department of a health insurance company. Elaine and her husband have made their home in Denver, CO. Two of their adult children live nearby, two live in Seattle and one in Reston, VA. She has a love of cooking and gardening passed along by her Mom and a passion for storytelling inherited from her Dad.

CPSIA information can be obtained
at www.ICGtesting.com
Printed in the USA
BVHW072123080621
609007BV00008B/1100